USA TODAY BESTSELLING AUTHOR

Dale Mayer

TERK'S GUARDIANS
LEGEND 02

LEGEND: TERK'S GUARDIANS, BOOK 2
Beverly Dale Mayer
Valley Publishing Ltd.

ISBN-13: 978-1-773367-95-8
Print Edition

Books in This Series:

About This Book

When Legend sees his political war-mongering father heading in a direction Legend can't agree with, he walks, but walking away from his little brother, Larry, can't happen. He is special in so many ways—even Clary, who has helped him many times, agrees. When intel of a government uprising is confirmed, Legend swoops in to remove Larry from the danger zone. It's not like Legend can leave behind his brother's tutor either …

Blair has been looking after Larry for years and had expected her position to continue for much longer, but, when Legend races in, barking orders to leave, her calm future is in sudden jeopardy. Nothing is easy or calm about Legend when he's around her.

As the coup fails, Legend's simple escape plan deteriorates quickly, and Larry's existence is suddenly a prize for cohorts, who haven't been paid and who are looking for a quick escape route too. Not that Blair would let anyone hurt her charge—even if it means dealing with and cooperating with the very irritating Legend.

Sign up to be notified of all Dale's releases here!
https://geni.us/DaleNews

PROLOGUE

TERK SAT AT the massive table, but the team was already trying to figure out how much bigger to make this seating arrangement. Terk stared at the table. "Can you imagine that we would need something even bigger than this?? There's already, what? Sixteen of us?"

"That's not something I thought would happen," Gage replied. "At least not so soon."

"Right." Terk smiled. "The thing is, we've done very well."

"What about Radar?"

"Well, … Radar will be coming on when he's ready. He needs a bit of training," Terk noted, "but that will be true for anybody who isn't in our team already."

"Right. So we'll need to potentially have somebody else coming on board to help out. What about Riff?"

"Riff is a world unto himself," Terk noted. "He did a great job helping out and being in the right spot at the right time."

"What about the woman who called you? Did she call back?"

"The sister to Riff's dead fiancée? She only phoned once," he said. "And I suspect she'll be here soon enough, whether we like it or not."

"Her energy is strong, isn't it?"

"Absolutely, but when she does get here, she'll be a force we'll have to deal with."

"And dealing with her won't be easy, especially if she's set on helping Riff with his problem."

"Riff will be in and out, at least for the next little while anyway," Terk shared. "He's got a lead on something, but he'll be back. So, if we need him on the next job, we just have to tag him, and he'll show up."

"He seems to do that a lot, doesn't he? Come and go, I mean."

"It's part of who he is, but, at the same time, he's somebody we desperately need to call on when we have problems."

"What about the billing aspect of this first MI6 job?" Celia asked, as she joined Terk at the table. "What did Jonas do with that?"

"Not only did we get a bonus for saving the government agents but, because of the double bombings and the other aspects that went into it that were outside the scope of the original assignment, our expenses are completely covered. Plus we got an extra 17 percent on top of all that, according to the calculations I worked out. They didn't even quibble," Terk added.

"Does that make you wonder if you've charged enough?" she asked in a teasing voice.

"Of course it does." He gave his wife a smirk. "I tossed it back and forth with Ice, and she confirmed that it was a really nicely paid job and to ensure we do everything we can to keep MI6 in our pocket because that level of job doesn't come by all the time."

"No, and that'll be something we want to encourage then," Celia noted, "because we're running through the cash pretty quickly, especially if we're saving for our own satellite."

"That is an understatement," Terk replied. "As we start trying to get some of these higher-level things in place, we'll need to set up some ongoing budgeting."

"Exactly, and there'll be an awful lot of people here, depending on the time frame that's needed just to get that satellite."

"Also"—Terk eyed the twin sisters with their special healing abilities heading toward the big dining table—"when Sammy gets here, she's been injured."

At that, both sisters nodded. "Yes, we've already been working on those injuries," Cara shared. "That deepest cut is pretty well healed and should be good to go. With this many people going back and forth all the time, our energies could get split up pretty easily."

"You can't wear yourselves down either," Terk warned, looking at them quite sternly.

They just smiled. Clary replied, "You also know that healing others helps us heal ourselves, so that's not really anything to worry about."

"Maybe not," he conceded, "but apparently I'm worrying enough for all of you." He pointed at their obviously pregnant states.

The twins burst out laughing at that. "Maybe," Cara admitted, "but who knew you would be such a worrisome dad."

"I didn't even think I could be," Terk admitted, with a headshake. "Yet this whole scenario has absolutely blown me away."

"All of us, actually," Celia noted, with a gentle smile for her husband. "But, as long as we don't have any other jobs at the moment, we should be good."

Just then Terk's phone rang. He looked down at it and frowned. "Terk here." The voice at the other end was one he knew but from a long time ago. "Jeremy, what the hell?" At the sound of an old friend, Terk smiled into the phone. "What's up? ... What do you mean?" he asked, listening to Jeremy ramble. "Hang on, hang on. Let me put this on Speakerphone, so the rest of the team can hear."

"You have a team?" Jeremy asked, with audible relief. "I heard you were done with the CIA."

"Yeah, but we've set up in the private sector."

"Thank God for that," he said. "As you well know, I'm still in the damn black ops business, but two of our teams have been taken, and we need you to do a reconnaissance mission. I'm presuming you can still stay where you are for that."

"I don't know whether we can or not. You'll have to give us a whole lot more information than that. And, if we have to send somebody, we'll send somebody. I do have some available people on our team who could go," he added, yet frowning as he looked around at everybody.

"I have one man in particular I need to bring back," Jeremy stated, "but he's injured, and I can tell you that he's damn good at what he does, but he took a blast, and I'm not sure what kind of ... it's somebody you know."

"Yeah, who's that?"

"Legend. The last we heard, he was attacked, and, after that, we lost contact. We don't know if he's alive or dead."

"Holy shit." Terk pinched the bridge of his nose. "He was unparalleled in his field."

"Yeah, and he has some of that weird stuff that you do, but we've had no communication from him. So, if you have any way of tracking where he is, just give us a location, so we can retrieve him. I really want to get him back again."

"Why is that?" Terk asked, hating the suspicion evident in his tone. "We will likely need to be involved."

Jeremy frowned and then said, "You might as well know it all. We're wondering if he was involved right from the beginning. As in for the wrong side. Others are grumbling about treason, but I don't want to believe it …"

"Absolutely no way," Terk declared.

"Good," Jeremy replied, "then prove it. We're hiring you and your team to get him and maybe, if needed, to prove that he's innocent because otherwise, as far as we can tell, that best friend of yours is guilty as hell."

CHAPTER 1

*T*ERKEL?

A forceful notice slammed into Terkel's brain. He straightened, dropping the stack of papers in his hands and looking around. "Clary?" There was no sign of her. Of course not. She wasn't in England.

Yes, it's me.

"What's the matter?" Terk asked out loud. Celia, sitting at his side, going over more stacks of papers, looked over at him, one eyebrow raised. He shook his head to let her know that it didn't involve her—at least he didn't think so.

No, it doesn't, Clary confirmed, able to follow his thoughts, *but we've got a problem.*

"We?"

She hesitated. *Well, I would say I have a problem. However, as I'm now part of a team,* she explained, her tone hardening, *I'll assume—and rightfully so, I think—that we have a problem.*

Terk nodded. "Fair enough. What's the problem?" He could almost feel some of her tension relaxing. "Does Brody know?"

No, ... and I would just as soon he didn't.

At that, Brody broke into the conversation. *Well, that's just too damn bad,* he snapped in Terkel's head.

Clary groaned. *It would help a lot if you wouldn't interfere in conversations that were not your own.*

Then pick another damn frequency, Brody declared, his tone equally hard. *You do remember this is the distress call signal?*

There was a moment of silence between the newlyweds.

Terkel gently slid his fingers through Celia's, as she telepathically joined in on the conversation too.

Clary groaned. *Damn. Fine. My bad. Still, I want it known that this doesn't involve you, Brody.*

If you've got a problem, it involves me, Brody stated. *You were supposed to go for a quick visit to check up on this patient of yours. What happened?*

What do you mean, what happened? Clary asked, her tone aggrieved, realizing she would have to involve him after all.

Terkel tried to pour oil onto troubled waters. "We are a team, Clary, and that includes Brody."

"Yes, and he's not up to full strength, but he'll still want to come racing over here to bail me out."

At that, Terkel winced because he already heard Brody's roar through his brain. "Brody, shut it down," Terk said, turning and seeing the wince on Celia's face. "Remember how this *is* the distress line. Everybody's getting slammed with that outcry of yours."

After several moments of harsh breathing, Brody finally relented. *Fine.* His tone backed down a few notches.

That's not helpful, Brody, Clary noted, her tone soft. *That's one of the reasons I didn't want to tell you.*

"Are you hurt? Are you in danger?" Terkel asked, before Brody had a chance.

She hesitated, then said, *Not hurt. Don't think I'm in danger.*

That's not a no, Brody snapped.

No, it sure isn't. Clary hesitated again. *No, I'm pretty sure he won't hurt me.*

"And again," Terkel added, his voice calm but curious, "that's not a no. Things in our world can just as quickly turn very ugly, so you may be in danger. Why don't you start at the beginning and let us know what is going on?"

She began with a warning, *Brody has to stay calm.*

Terkel's lips twitched. "Yeah, well, Brody has a bit of a volcanic temper when it comes to you, so, Brody, you'll do your best to stay calm, won't you?"

Of course, he bit off.

At that, Terk caught Celia's big grin. He rolled his eyes at her. "Look, Clary. We just need some details. Then maybe we can do some research and see what's going on."

I came to see little Larry, she replied. *Remember? He was one of my previous patients. At four years old, I helped bring him back from the edge of death, and that was a good five to six years ago.*

"And?" Terk prodded.

So I came for his checkup, gave him another dose of healing to hold him for a while, and he is holding. That's the good news, she confirmed, yet in an anxious tone.

"But?" Terk asked.

But something is going on in his psyche, and I think it's coming from somebody else. Maybe something to do with his father.

"Explain."

His father is a Kazak national, living with Larry in Azerbaijan, she explained. *Although I'm not there. Not yet. I was in France with another patient. However, I flew back to Larry. The car will drop me off in just a few minutes. I'm ... I'm feeling hooks, some serious energy coming from his direction.*

"Go on," Terkel said, continuing in the same calm vein. "Why does this involve us?"

Because I believe that the father has enemies who are trying to keep his son ill, through energy negativity.

"When you say negativity, what does that mean to you?"

I think somebody, like us, is using it to harm and to cause chaos instead of good.

"Well, for whatever light is out there, we also know there is darkness," Terkel noted, "so that's possible, but again, if this has something to do with us, why?"

Because his father is suddenly aware that maybe something is going on with his son, and he's asked me if there's something I can do to stave off an attack.

"What kind of an attack?"

I think energy-related, but I'm not sure, Clary replied, her voice gaining confidence as she spoke and described it. *I think there'll be a kidnapping attempt, and I think that this energy will be used to help them. When I say* them, *I mean whoever is involved in this attack will stay under cover of darkness and will spirit the boy away.*

"And will that kill him?" Terk asked.

No, he's been functioning on his own just fine for quite a few years. However, I'm seeing something wrong in his energy. I just can't really describe what I'm seeing because I haven't had enough time yet to really investigate. But I am certain that it's not good, she added for emphasis.

"Okay, but you're thinking this is involved with whatever the attack is?"

I think so, but I can't be sure, she murmured.

Terkel went silent for a moment. "What does the father say?"

He says the budget is unlimited, she repeated in a dry

tone.

At that, Tasha spoke up. "Good, that one's for us then," she said bluntly. "We're bleeding money at an incredible rate, trying to get everything set up. So the answer is absolutely yes. We can help."

"But can we?" Terkel asked. "Stepping up and helping is one thing, and I have no problem doing that, but we have to know that we can actually enact some good here."

At that, Brody, his voice now somewhat calmer, asked, *How imminent do you think this attack is?*

When Clary hesitated, Terkel knew another blowup was coming. *Brody,* he said in a warning tone of voice.

He sighed. *I'm listening, and I won't blow up.*

Well, you probably will, Clary noted quietly, *because I suspect it'll be in the next forty-eight hours.*

Come home, Brody demanded.

Well, coming home doesn't save this little boy, and he's … I don't know how to explain it, but I think Terkel would understand.

"I do understand," Terk replied. "If they kill Larry, you're connected to him, aren't you, Clary?"

Yes, she agreed, her voice faint. *Can I disconnect? Well, that is possible, but I just don't know how hard it'll be or how dangerous, for Larry or for me.*

"It'll be very dangerous," Terkel stated, "particularly if this boy—who is what, ten or so now?—if he is connected to you or if you are connected to him to the depths of the edge of death."

Yes, he's definitely connected to me, she said, her voice catching on a sob. *We've been very close ever since.*

"Of course you have," Terk muttered, his voice softening. "And now somebody you love is in danger."

What about somebody I love? Brody snapped. *Because what you're saying is, if that boy dies, I'll lose her too, aren't you?*

Maybe not in the sense that you're thinking of it, Clary added, *but it's possible that I could lose myself to the ethers, caught between here and there, and/or possibly dead.*

In that case, Tasha joined in telepathically, her voice calm, *that just underlines why we're doing this. We are a team, and we protect our own.*

Terkel nodded absentmindedly, but his mind was already considering the logistics.

When the father says unlimited, he means unlimited. This is his beloved son, Clary shared. *There's also another element.*

At that, Terkel winced. "There's always another element, it seems."

He has a bastard son.

"Okay, and that's an issue, why?"

Because I think he has a lot of energy skills as well.

"Now that's also interesting, but he's an issue, why?"

I'm not sure he is an issue. I just can't get a read on him. It's as if his energy is completely locked down, and I can't tell one way or the other if he's on our side or throwing in with the other side. It could be his energy at play causing the problem with Larry.

"Is anybody there you would consider an enemy?"

Somebody else is around Larry, and I'm not sure if she's an enemy. It's not often that I meet people I can't read, but Blair is definitely one of them.

"What's her relationship to the little boy?"

She's his nanny.

"Okay, and do you see a love connection?"

Absolutely. Larry is very attached to her, and then, of course, as soon as I got there, that opened to include me. It's not that it wasn't there to begin with. It just was under cover. Well, under the cover of energy, yes, she added, with a half laugh. *Do you realize how absolutely bizarre it is to even talk to you about this?*

"And yet it's a blessing that we are here and that we can talk about it," Terk reminded her.

I'm working on that reminder, she admitted. *So his father is requesting or is planning on requesting, so I mean it shouldn't come through me, but some assistance ...*

"What is it he's requesting?"

That we keep the boy safe.

"We don't do security work," he reminded her. "At least not bodyguard level."

I'm not sure that this is security that anybody else can do, Clary noted. *This is definitely a case of somebody having an advantage here and utilizing it to possibly hurt this little boy.*

There was silence on the channel, and then Terkel said, "Brody?"

I'm going. I've already packed my bag. Such a note of finality filled his tone that there was absolutely no point in arguing.

"Your job ..."

Is to protect Clary, Brody stated. At that, he spoke to his wife. *Clary, what's the name of this man, this bastard son? Have you got any idea what's going on with him?*

Only that there is some level of familiarity, Clary replied, *and I only know his first name.*

What is it?

Legend. His name is Legend.

At that, Terkel closed his eyes, but a smile played around the corner of his lips. *Damn. Now that couldn't be a coincidence.*

Seriously? Is Legend involved in this? Brody asked in shock.

Clary spoke up, *Who is Legend?*

Legend is, … well, Legend.

Do you know him? Clary asked Brody. *I didn't say he was* involved, *involved. I just said that he's a man of power somewhere in the picture, and I just don't know how, where, or what.*

At that comment came a call on Terkel's phone. He looked down at it and started to laugh. "I don't know whether it's your boy's father or someone else," Terk told them all, "but I'm getting a call, so give me a minute." Then he quickly disconnected from their telepathic distress channel.

CHAPTER 2

LEGEND STARED DOWN at his damn phone. Terk was always busy. Sometimes almost impossible to get through to. As if on purpose. "Answer, will you?" he muttered in frustration. But instead, Terkel's voice slammed into his brain.

Well, I would, but maybe you should be answering your own calls.

Legend shifted in his armchair and stared up at the ceiling. "Do you always have to be unconventional?" he called out to the empty room.

It saves time and energy.

"*This* takes a lot of energy," Legend snapped. Still he laid his back against one of the high wingbacks and smiled. There was none like Terk. Never would be anyone again.

Terkel laughed. *Well, it does require lots of energy, unless you learn how to portion it off.*

"Yeah, well, I've never been very good at that."

No, you and Brody have always been more like steamrollers when it came to energy.

"Brody? As in the Brody I know?"

Yeah, that Brody.

"Well, shit. I would ask you all kinds of good questions about him and a few other people we know in common," he began, "but I don't have time. I've got a problem."

Yeah, you do. Your little half-brother Larry is in trouble.

There was shock on the other end. "What the hell?" he snapped.

Clary, Terkel stated carefully, *is part of my team.*

After another moment of absolute shock, Legend started to laugh. "What the hell? Of course she is. Jesus Christ, is she really as good as my father says?"

Ah, yeah, every bit and more, Terk confirmed, *and, yes, she brought your little brother back from death some five years or so ago.*

"Good God," Legend muttered, shaking his head at the thought. "You know how you hear about something like that, and, being an energy wielder myself, you wonder just how far we can take this, but I just had no …" Then his voice dropped off. He shook his head, as he continued to stare at the ceiling. "So, where do we stand?"

That's a good question, Terk noted. *I gather you also have problems.*

"My father has made a lot of enemies," Legend said, his voice harsh. "I've done a lot to stay out of the problems, but, once it involved Larry, that became a whole different story."

I understand, Terkel replied. *Larry's been through a lot.*

"He's been through too damn much. The kid just wants to have a normal life, but it seems impossible to give it to him."

How is his health now?

"Perfect. I mean, whatever Clary did, or is doing, seems to be one hell of a magic potion," he muttered. "I just wish I understood from what level she was doing it."

I already told you, Terk reminded him.

"Yeah, I know. I'm still getting my brain wrapped around it though. My father is very involved in politics and the government—and not necessarily the current government," he snapped.

At that, Terkel winced. *Right, so he's made some powerful enemies, which legally are probably in the right.*

More silence then Legend said, "As much as anybody over here with the current government is in the right, but yes. According to the existing powers that be, whatever my father is doing is getting him and the family in deep shit."

Anybody else in the family?

"No, not alive anymore. Both my mother, whom he never married, and his first wife passed away several years ago. His second wife walked away, and, when Larry got so sick, his third wife committed suicide." Now came silence on the other end of his brain.

So, this little boy's been to hell and back. So, what is it you think you need?

"I need backup and help. I wasn't necessarily thinking of strong-arm type people, but potentially …"

How are your skills? Terkel asked, only half curious, suspecting that he knew the answer.

"Top-notch of course," Legend stated. "Knowing where my father's interests lie, I can always be a target so can't let my guard down—even with my own team. Once people find out the familial connection, it will be a shit show. So, most people don't know, and I like to keep it that way."

Are you close to your father?

"Hell no, not after my mother passed away, especially since I highly suspect it was because of him. I don't have time for that kind of emotional turmoil, and, while the world's gone to hell in a handbasket, I'm just doing my part to stay sane and to keep little Larry safe. But I also work, so some of this came up suddenly, when I wasn't expecting it.

You may have heard rumors already, of my capture and escape. Neither is true. I just needed to get free and to get to Larry without encumbrances. Whether we survive this or we kill ourselves off in the next Ice Age, I don't know."

Sounds like that Ice Age is coming a whole lot faster than we expect.

"Whatever it is, there sure as hell is something going on here. My skills are up-to-date. I'm just not sure how many people I'm up against, and I can't have eyes everywhere. But if Clary is one of yours …"

Clary is definitely one of mine, and her partner is on the way to you right now to help her, as well as to help you.

There was a moment of shock, as images filtered through Legend's head, and then he laughed. "Good God, Brody married to Clary? Bullish Brody?"

Yeah, and believe me, they make a heck of a pair.

"Well, Clary's never struck me as a pushover," Legend shared, "at least not the few times I've met her. But couldn't Brody stay where you are and help out?"

No way you'll keep Brody from Clary right now, Terkel noted.

"Fine," Legend replied in resignation. "I'm not too sure just what the hell's going on here, so he's walking into an ugly situation."

He's used to that, and we're always on the ready and available to help him out.

"Does that help extend to me?'

If you need it, yes. I've been trying to get you to come work for us for a long time.

"Yeah, about that. I'll never be government material," he admitted. "You know that."

No, but what you should probably know is that we're pri-

vate now.

"You're what?" Now that was a shock. He'd been concerned that Terk was government in the first place but yet felt it was okay in some way that Legend couldn't explain.

Yeah, it's a long story that I don't have time to share right now because I'll obviously need to jump in on this case, but, if we help you, I hope you'll consider coming to work for me here.

"Well shit," Legend muttered, finding all his former arguments without the same merit as they would have had before.

We'll talk about it later, Terkel said. *Right now, you've got enough problems.*

"Yes, I've got to get Larry out of here."

What about his nurse? Terkel asked. *Or babysitter, or nanny, or whatever she is?*

At that, Legend's voice changed. "Yeah, then there's *her,*" he said, his tone suddenly hard.

What does that mean?

"I don't know exactly what role she's playing here. I don't really know anything about this. As far as I know, she's yet another innocent who'll get crushed by my father's politics," Legend muttered. Yet he also knew more about her than he should. At least his heart did. He'd taken a short walk down that direction—enough to know the sweetest of kisses and so much more awaited but also knowing his brother needed Blair at such a deep level that Legend had chosen to back off. In the ensuing years she'd been sniping at him ever since. He understood but remained adamant.

Well, you might want to consider that she may need a quick exit too.

"Right, so now we're running a nanny service, are we?" He winced because no way would he leave her behind regardless. She likely had no idea what was going on right now either. He hadn't told her, and no way his father would have either.

It's not like you to leave her behind anyway.

"I wasn't planning on it," he replied in disgust. "But she ..."

She what?

"She irritates the hell out of me," he snapped. That much was true. And then he added, "Tell Brody to get in contact when he lands in Azerbaijan. I don't want him coming to the house unannounced. He's likely to get shot." And, with that, Legend disconnected from Terkel.

Legend stared out the window for a long moment, then shook his head. "Well, hell." On the inside though, he felt a measurable chill. It was one thing to deal with all the shit going on alone, and he would handle it because no way he wouldn't handle it, but to know that Clary was part of Terkel's team was huge. Now he really wanted to pick her brain about how that had come about and what the hell she was doing with Larry, and for him, but that conversation would have to wait.

Whether she knew that Brody was on his way or not, she needed to know more problems were going on than she actually understood, and Legend would have to be the one to tell her. On that note he got up and headed into the other room, looking for her.

As he walked into the playroom, where Larry liked to hang out during the day, Legend found it completely empty. Frowning, he stepped forward and looked out over the gardens but still no sign of Larry. Legend closed his eyes and sent out a probe, something that he'd managed to do quite a few times since he had learned to lock down his own energy.

He noted energy and more than one source coming from Larry's bedroom. With that, he turned on a fast trot to confirm that the little boy was okay.

BLAIR LOOKED UP at Legend's sudden arrival and glared. "According to Mr. Kartal, you're not welcome here." Legend didn't even give her a worthy glance. She stepped up beside her charge.

Larry reached out a hand and squeezed her fingers, adding, "It's fine." He looked up at Legend. "Is it time?"

Legend's eyebrows shot up. "Time for what?"

"To leave," Larry said simply.

Legend glanced over at Clary, who stood quietly on the other side of the room, studying him with a knowing look. He shrugged.

"It's obvious something's going on," Clary noted. "Now, seeing you, … it means trouble."

Legend sighed. "We have some visitors coming. I was hoping to wait until they arrived, but maybe it's better if we leave now." He asked Clary, "How close is Brody?"

She winced. "Brody should be here fairly quickly," she noted, with an eye roll.

"Of course he will."

Clary looked down at Larry, ignoring Legend. "Maybe we should go pack you a bag."

"That's a good idea," Larry agreed but turned to Blair. "Do you want to do my clothes? I'll pack up my school books instead."

At that, knowing she'd been dismissed but unsure why Legend was involved, Blair turned and headed to Larry's closet. She quickly took out a suitcase and started packing several outfits.

"Cut it in half," Legend said from the doorway. "Backpacks only. I don't know how hard our run will be."

She stiffened and turned to face him. She masked her expression quickly and nodded.

Legend walked to the closet, pulled out a large backpack, and noted, "Something like this will work."

She didn't say a word because there was absolutely no point in wasting the energy. When Legend spoke, he tended to expect everybody to jump instead of asking how high, not even bothering to be polite, presuming they would be told what they needed on the way. She didn't do so well with that regimented attitude, but her job meant following orders, so she packed what would be clothes for a week, surprised at how quickly the rucksack didn't fill up. "It's surprisingly large," she muttered, but Legend was not bothered.

"He's a little boy. His clothes are small."

She nodded, then went over and grabbed his chargers and packed them up for his tablet and his phone.

At that, Legend said, "Phone only."

"He uses his tablet for a lot of his schoolwork."

Legend hesitated, then nodded. "Fine."

Then she went into the bathroom, grabbed the basics for his personal hygiene—toothbrush, toothpaste. When she came back out again, the bag was still surprisingly empty. She grabbed the book that he had been reading and looked around. "Is he allowed a second rucksack for his schoolwork?"

At that, Legend nodded. "School is important to him, isn't it?"

"He lost a lot of time," she replied smoothly. "So, he's

been working hard to catch up again."

"In four years he hasn't caught up?" he asked.

"He has caught up and exceeded," she proudly admitted, "but he won't appreciate it if I tell you that."

"Why?"

"His father doesn't look at his educational aspirations with any fondness," she murmured, "and, of course, there's always the chance that you'll go tattle."

At that, his gaze narrowed, and his lips thinned.

She gave him a sunny smile. "You did once."

"Hardly. That was different, and you know it."

She shrugged. "Not to him." Okay, so maybe not quite true, but Legend had told Larry's father that Blair was too interested in Larry and that that gotten her a dressing down from Mr. Kartal, blaming her for keeping his son away from him. It was partly true, but Blair and Legend had made a decision to not move forward with a relationship for Larry's sake.

It had hurt at the time, but every time since it had been worse. It should have gotten easier over time, but it hadn't. She tended to get snippy and irritated when Legend was around. Not because of what he'd reported to his father—which she couldn't trust his version of the truth either—but because she still cared for Legend and knew that he cared for her too. And that pissed her off. Big-time.

She walked back out to the classroom that they used for his studies to find Larry standing there, with a stack of books essentially too big for his bag.

"There's a little bit of room in this one," Blair offered.

Larry saw that and grinned, quickly stuffing the rest of his books into it, making sure his tablet was in there. "Did you get my charger?" he asked impatiently.

"Yes, and seven days of clothes, but …" She quickly re-membered something and raced back into his bedroom, grabbed his favorite pajamas, and returned to the classroom, where she stuffed the PJs into the bag as well.

Clary looked over at her. "You've probably got about thirty minutes to grab your stuff." Clary's tone was plain and final.

"You too?" Blair asked Clary.

"Yes, I'm doing the same."

Leaving Larry with Legend, the two women split. Blair headed to her room, where she probably had more than a backpack full but knew she would leave behind the rest. She didn't bring much in the way of clothing, as she kept to more of a uniform attire every day. Then, on the weekends, when she was supposedly allowed free time, she didn't actually get free time because she was looking after Larry all the time, so she preferred jeans.

She quickly packed her jeans and left the uniforms be-hind, realizing that she had almost nothing. Such a scarcity of any clothing was in her backpack, since she'd never added much to what she'd originally brought. Thus it all fit in, as long as she left behind the work clothing. With that out of the way, she quickly grabbed her chargers, her tablet, and her laptop, her bag now stuffed to the point that it would be hard to close.

Managing to get it closed, she headed back to the class-room and added her bag to the other two sitting there on the floor. Clary's was there within seconds of hers.

Blair turned, looked at Larry, ignoring Legend, and asked, "What says his majesty now?" She was obviously referring to Legend.

Larry shrugged. "Legend says he's waiting for somebody."

"Of course he is." At that, she turned, glared at Legend, and asked, "Did your *friend* contact you yet?"

He shook his head. "Not yet."

Blair eyed him, catching him wince, as something slammed into his brain. She looked over at Clary to see a smile sliding through her face. "Obviously you guys know something I don't," Blair noted, "but I will arrange for outerwear and shoes, just in case. Come on, Larry." And, with that, she grabbed two of the backpacks, while Larry grabbed his schoolbooks, wincing under the weight. She quickly traded him for the lighter pack, threw the schoolbooks over her shoulder, and said, "Let's get shoes."

"I guess we're only bringing one pair of shoes," Larry muttered. "We don't have room for anything else."

"I have a little more room in mine," Clary offered behind them. Larry nodded, with a big smile.

Down at the front door, Blair opened the coat closet, grabbed her jacket, the only one she had brought with her, noting that Clary had grabbed hers, then Blair assessed the outerwear choices for Larry. He still got cold a lot, yet she didn't know if they would spend much time outside.

However, Larry took the decision away from her by grabbing a jacket with sleeves and a lining that could be zipped out, if need be. It was warm but could be very versatile. He put that over his arm, as he stared at the closet. "I'll take my sneakers," he announced, grabbing them. He sat on the nearby bench seat and quickly put them on.

Blair watched his energy, but he constantly surprised her at how well he handled different situations. She didn't understand in many ways, but, since meeting Clary, a lot of it had become more obvious. Clary stood at the front door, and Legend was still in the middle of the great hall, waiting for them to finish packing. Blair turned, looked from Clary to Legend, and asked, "Which way?"

Legend pointed. "This way."

Clary rounded on him. "Not yet."

Blair sighed. "Anytime you two want to tell me what's going on, it would be nice."

"We will," Clary replied, "just not yet."

And that was as good as it would get. Blair looked down at Larry to see him tying off his shoes. Then he bounced to his feet and shouldered his backpack, then walked over to Legend and stood at his side.

Looking back at the women, Larry asked, "Are you guys coming?" They were both very important elements in his life, the only two women he had any kind of relationship with, and, in both cases, each was warm, caring, and strong. Blair looked over at Clary, who was leaning against the door, but the look on her face was one of concentration. "How long?" Blair asked Clary.

She looked up, smiled, and replied, "Ten minutes."

"Ten minutes, okay then." Blair now sat on the entry-way bench, quickly rearranged a few items in the backpack she was carrying, and managed to add a heavier pair of shoes for Larry. He loved the ones that he had on, but they wouldn't hold up to heavy running. Then, if she had to carry these backpacks, she wouldn't hold up all that long either. Though she had a few tricks up her sleeve to make that happen too. She walked over to Legend and handed him the spare backpack. He quickly picked it up, shouldered it, and she realized he didn't have a bag of his own. "Do you not have any belongings here?"

He shrugged. "Everything I need, I can pick up somewhere else."

She nodded, then turned back to Clary, who was holding up one hand, all her fingers splayed, then folding down a thumb, the next finger, three, two, one, and the door opened silently beside her.

The man who stepped in entered with such force, yet his movements were calm and subtle.

Blair stared at him, then looked at Clary, who turned to her with a chuckle.

"Right on time."

The man strode to Clary, picked her up in his arms in a bear hug, and, after kissing her thoroughly, he kept her behind him and walked over to Legend, where the two monster-men stood staring at each other, sharing hard glances.

Blair's jaw dropped, as she studied the silent war going on between them.

Clary smiled at Blair and explained, "It's fine." Then Clary turned to her husband. "He's fine, Brody."

Blair stared at both men, wide-eyed. "Sure it's fine, as long as you're okay with the war of the Titans."

"There's no war," Clary noted. "The conquest has already happened. He has his queen, and, as long as everybody else knows that, he'll be fine."

With that, Blair understood what was going on and started to laugh. She walked past Legend, smacked him hard on the shoulder, and said, "Let's get the show on the road." Then, with a smile, she headed to the basement exit that she already knew about. Everyone silently followed.

They had yet to know that the current battle had just begun.

CHAPTER 3

B LAIR RACED DOWN the stairs, quickly being overtaken by Legend. She stopped to see that Larry was trying hard to keep up. He was right between Clary and Brody. Blair hadn't had much chance to assess the man, but he kept very close to Clary. Blair smiled at Clary. as they caught up. "How does it feel to be part of a strong-man competition?"

Clary rolled her eyes. "He's just protective, that's all," she muttered.

"You called me, saying you were in trouble," Brody declared. "What did you expect?"

"No, I called Terkel," she corrected, then smiled up at him, "but you're welcome to stay as long as you want."

"Why not call me directly?" he asked, looking at her in confusion.

"Because, if I'd called you, you would have been in much worse shape."

He sighed. "You're the only one who makes me turn stupid like that," he muttered.

"That's because you love me," she noted.

He gave a curt nod. "That I do." And he kissed her long and hard.

The exchange was sincere, passionate, and hot, and Blair was charmed. A man who could admit he was silly and sick with love over a good woman made him a great man in

Blair's book.

As Blair caught up to Legend, he looked back at the pair and muttered, "If you guys are done …"

Clary chuckled. "Your time will come."

"Yeah, I can wait," Legend replied in exasperation. "Do we have a timeline, Clary?"

"Five minutes. I'm expecting them already."

"I passed one vehicle broken down on the road," Brody shared, "and, when I ditched my vehicle and hid it in the brush, I heard a fair bit of arguing soon afterward."

At that, Legend looked at him in surprise. "You passed them?"

He shrugged. "I might have."

Legend narrowed his gaze. "Might have?"

"Yes, might have," Brody growled. "It's not as if I've got any idea who you're after or who's after you, potentially after all of us now."

"No, of course not," Legend agreed.

Knowing that something substantial was happening that nobody had thought to let her in on, Blair walked over to Larry and asked him, "You ready for this?"

He shrugged. "Why not? I mean, all I can do is die." Then he laughed, adding, "Again."

"Doesn't mean I can save you again," Clary declared, her tone firm. "So don't do anything foolish."

Blair looked back at Clary and admitted, "Larry's mentioned that several times."

Clary nodded. "Despite the fact that he knows he's not supposed to." She faced Larry in warning, who, while abashed, still nodded.

"I'm sorry, Clary," he said. "It's just, well, it's a rather delicious story."

She chuckled. "It is, indeed, but remember? Not everybody understands, and that puts a certain level of danger out there that we don't want. Particularly for me."

"I get it," Larry agreed.

"Well, if you got it," Legend snapped, "you wouldn't be saying it."

Immediately Larry's face fell.

Blair looked over at Legend and frowned. "Stop picking on him," Blair declared.

Legend groaned. "Why is reminding him of this, *picking on him?*"

"Because it wasn't for you to do, and he'd already been corrected," Blair explained in exasperation. "Better to let it go."

"Well, look at you, Miss Perfect, in the raising of kids. He needs to really *get it,* get it, and, if you like kids so much," he stared at her, one eyebrow raised, "why don't you go have your own?"

"If I thought any man left on this planet was worth using for a sperm donor, I might consider it," she snapped back.

At that came a moment of silence, and Brody started to laugh and laugh and laugh. "Oh my God," he said, in between fits of laughter, "it's happening, isn't it?" He looked over at Clary, who just gave him a wink and a nod. "Wow, even here."

"I won't even ask what that means." Blair glared at the two of them. "Considering you've all chosen to leave here, we need to have some serious conversations when we get back."

"Yeah, you're not kidding," Brody noted, with a wry look.

"Conversations about what?" Legend asked, as he opened up the exit door in front of him.

"Did you actually do a run to make sure nobody was hiding out here?" Blair asked, ignoring his question. Besides he likely already knew the answer.

"Yes, when I last checked, nobody was there. Right now though, I can't tell you that it remains safe because it's taken so long to get you guys this far."

"Well, that was a matter of getting Brody here," Blair pointed out, looking back at Brody. "Not that we were expecting him."

"Well, seeing as how I disabled their car," Brody replied, "you're welcome."

Legend gave a short snort at that. "Well then, let's get the hell out of here, before they make up for lost time." And he quickly stepped out and made a quick scan of the area and then pulled out Blair, followed by Larry, with Clary and Brody bringing up the rear. The door was closed and locked behind them.

Brody stepped up beside Legend. "Split up or stay to-gether?"

"Yeah, that's a problem. I suggest we stay together."

Clary's voice came crisp and clear. "We're staying to-gether. Absolutely no way we're splitting up." Then she glared at the two men. "So you just get that through your heads right now." And, with that, she put an arm around Larry's shoulders, reached out a hand toward Blair, and said, "Come on." She led the way forward, leaving the men to bring up the rear.

Blair laughed. "At least you know how to deal with them."

"Yeah, you will learn quickly. They're much like children," she snapped, and then she laughed. "But now you can understand where they come from and why."

"Got it," Blair noted. "I thought that was more of a discussion though."

"Sure it was, but it was also more of a testing to see who would come up with a better idea and with the proper reasoning."

"Hey, you know we're allowed to discuss things," Legend noted. Then he looked over at Brody. "Seriously? This is what you put up with all the time?"

"Absolutely. Or at least whenever I step sideways," he muttered.

At that, Legend started to laugh. "Wow, how the mighty has fallen."

"Says you. I don't consider it falling a bit."

"Of course not. You're *in love*."

But Legend said the words in such a twisted tone that Blair took umbrage. "Just because you've never been in love and have never cared for anybody but yourself, don't go mocking it."

"Whoa, whoa, whoa. Where did that come from?"

"Whatever," Blair muttered, with a casual wave of her hand. Legend pissed her off in ways she didn't want to examine too closely.

Almost immediately Clary grabbed Blair's hand. "Watch that thing. It's a weapon." Blair stared at her in surprise. "You don't realize," Clary added. "We so need to have a talk and soon."

"About what?"

"Keeping it in control," she murmured, her voice low. "It's hardly something we want to talk about right now, but, when you're upset, you can send out quite a punch."

"I know," she admitted. "And I *am* trying to keep it under control."

"You know?" Clary asked, looking at Blair with a searching gaze.

"To a certain extent. I'm just not, … not very good at it, … the control thing."

"*Umm-hmm*," Clary replied. "Anybody in particular send it flying?"

At that, Blair glared at her, knowing Clary was clearly laughing at her. "It's that obvious, *huh*?"

"Yeah, on both sides though," Clary noted cheerfully.

"Nothing is funny about all this."

Just then, a shot rang out. The men quickly urged them into the trees, where they were immediately sequestered.

"Was that just an aimless shot or did we get seen?" Blair asked.

"I think it was a shot within the mansion for a target within," Legend stated.

"Who was left inside?" Brody asked, looking at the women.

"The kitchen staff," Clary noted.

"The butler," Blair added shakily.

"Right, everybody was in there," Larry murmured quietly, and his bottom lip started to tremble.

"Easy, we don't know that there's been anything other than a warning shot fired," Legend stated in a quiet tone. "Let's not borrow trouble."

The boy took a deep breath and nodded. "They better not have hurt the butler. He's one of the good guys."

"Good," Clary added. "Then his life isn't in vain, is it?" At that, Larry turned and looked up at her, and she shook her head. "No, I won't take a look. I won't do anything at all at this point in time. I'm not getting any call for help, and I won't go help without that call. We have enough on our plates right now."

"But you can keep him alive."

"And she could get shot in the process," Brody added, his voice hard and unrelenting. "There are times, and there are places, plus we need an okay to go in that direction."

Larry wasn't easily convinced, but, by the time they had him moving again and a vehicle arranged to pick them up in a while, he was quiet.

"You also don't know that anything has actually happened to him," Clary said beside him.

"But you could check."

"I could, but it's energy that I'm not prepared to put out right now."

"Why not?" Larry asked, frowning at her.

"Because we're in danger, and I think somebody is tracking energy signatures. They're looking for us."

Larry frowned at her and shook his head. "How is that even a thing?"

"It's not only a thing, it's a done deal, and I'm not prepared to bring attention to us."

He sighed. "Will I ever learn how to do this?"

"Maybe. Do you want to?"

"Of course I want to, if for no other reason than to not be so vulnerable in this world that's so hell-bent on being nasty."

"Don't swear," Blair stated, but the boy just glared at her. She shrugged. "I get it, but you know there's no need for that kind of language while we're out here."

"Surely that's when the language should be okay," he snapped at her. Then he crossed his arms and continued to glare. She smiled at him. "It's not a sign of being in control to swear. It's a sign of being out of control."

"It's also a sign of letting off steam," Larry added, still glaring at her.

"That's fine, and, when I'm not under your father's orders to keep you from swearing, then that's something you can talk about, but, in the meantime, no swearing is part of my instructions."

"It's not fair," Larry grumbled. "Everybody else swears."

"When you are an adult, you can do what you want to do in that regard," Blair suggested, "but, for the moment, that's not the case. By the way, has anybody contacted his father?"

"Not yet," Legend replied. "I did talk to him last night, when I warned him that we were heading into ugly times."

"What did he say?"

"That he didn't believe me," he snapped.

"Of course he said that," Larry muttered under his breath. "He's trying to overthrow the government, so what does anybody care about but that?" At that, the adults turned and looked at him. "Do you really think I don't know what's going on or how my father feels about all this?"

Legend looked between him and Blair, then scanned the others and shook his head.

Larry continued. "It's not easy being a child, but it's even harder being *this* age, where everybody looks at you like you're some sort of a delicate wallflower and can't be trusted with anything," Larry shared bitterly. "Certainly not my father."

"Your father loves you," Blair told him softly. "Regardless of what happens, remember that."

"Just not enough to quit going to war."

"In his mind," Blair explained, "and I'm not saying he's right or wrong, but, in his mind, he's trying to help more than a few people and more than just his son."

At that, Larry frowned. "I wonder," he replied contemplatively. "Or is it just about money and power?"

"I'm sorry," Blair whispered. "Those are not questions that any ten-year-old should ask of his parents."

"Parents? I don't even know about the other half of my parentage," Larry muttered. "I figure that'll have to wait a few years, and then I'll assess whether I want to go deeper."

"You do that," Blair agreed. "Now, a lot of effort has gone into keeping you alive, so let's make sure that we continue to do that."

"But not just you," Larry pointed out. "Clary is the one who put all that effort in."

"And then," Clary interrupted, "you need to realize that Blair has done a hell of a job keeping you healthy and safe. She is the one looking after you day in and day out."

He groaned. "I'm not trying to be mean," he muttered.

Blair heard his tone break. She reached out her hand and said, "We know, sweetie. We all understand."

He put his hand in hers and squeezed. "I'm sorry," he whispered.

She smiled at him. "I'm not insulted. You're right, and it's okay."

"No, it's not okay," Larry apologized. "I didn't mean to make it sound like I didn't need you too, because I do."

"It's okay," Blair repeated firmly. "Life sometimes gives us surprises. It's up to us as to how we deal with them, even when they're not pleasant ones."

As Larry continued to walk in the woods away from his home, not knowing what was ahead of him, the fact that he was even cognizant of these real-world problems and capable of talking about any of it was amazing. But then, as Blair had come to discover, this little boy had an awful lot of amazing traits to offer the world.

He had a very philosophical attitude, one that his father did not understand in any way. If his father would say, *Go to war*, this little boy would say, *Why? Peace would make the world go round.* If his father would laugh at him, Larry would say, *You can laugh, but the world is not just your world. It's everybody's world.*

She'd been on the outside of many arguments Larry had had with his father, where she had been given a harsh tongue-lashing afterward, when Mr. Kartal had been unhappy at his son's ability to argue in a clear, concise manner, stating the error of his father's ways. Mr. Kartal had felt that his son should be following his own methodologies and thought processes, but it wasn't to be.

There was no way to brainwash this child who'd already been through so much, and, for that, Blair was grateful. Larry had already proven to have a sharp and creative mind of his own, along with a compassionate heart and so much else. He was a very special child, and Blair didn't want that beaten out of him, no matter how much his father wanted Larry to be there at his side when they overtook the capital. Because, in her heart of hearts, she didn't feel like taking the capital was a good idea to begin with and was no place for a child—certainly not *this* child.

But her personal political opinions weren't part of her nanny job, and not for the first time she did worry about the type of work she took on because she became so attached to the children who weren't her own. But, as Legend had reminded her, she should have her own. And, like her reply, the options for a perfect person for her were sadly lacking. She hadn't found anyone so far.

When they'd hiked for a good forty minutes, she stopped, looked at the others, and asked, "How much longer?" Larry looked up at her and smiled. She reached down, tousled his hair. "I knew you would ask that question, but I decided to jump in before you."

"And that's because you didn't want to make it look like I'm not doing so well." He laughed at her.

She smiled. "And here comes that wise old man locked inside that young body."

"Yet," he stated, staring at her intently. "It doesn't bother you?"

"After all these years? No, it doesn't bother me at all," she shared, "because I know the truth."

At that, Legend stepped forward and announced, "We have a vehicle meeting us just around the bend up here."

"Good enough," Blair replied and stepped back. "Go ahead and meet them." Legend frowned at her. "You go on ahead first," Blair instructed. "If anybody gets shot, it's you." He glared at her then, and she smiled. "I just don't want anything to happen to Larry."

"He's my brother, you know?" Legend snapped.

"He's your half-brother, from a father who hasn't recognized your lineage."

LEGEND STARED AT her, a muscle twitching in the corner of his mouth, as she gave him a flat stare right back. "That's quite true," he admitted, "publicly at least. Though my father is perfectly aware of who I am and what our relationship is."

She nodded. "Just so we're clear."

"You mean, clear that you don't trust me?" Then why would she?

"Clearly you have secrets that I'm not sure I can trust. Awfully insightful of you to see that," she muttered.

There was something about this woman; she just never backed down. Sometimes he wished she would. "As long as Brody is staying here with you, I will be quite happy to go check for our ride." Shooting her a hard glance, Legend issued a word of warning, "Look after my brother." Then he disappeared into the trees.

He stepped out to the side of the road but stayed hidden along embankments of rocks and watched. He'd been tracking the vehicle on his phone, knowing they were close, just not close enough. It was always the *not close enough* that bothered him. Particularly after hearing the shooting in the mansion. When he saw no sign of the vehicle, and its arrival time had come and gone, he sent out an alert, but there was nothing. Swearing at that, he quickly returned to the group and shook his head.

"The vehicle stopped tracking. I don't know where it is, but it's not coming. I've got no message saying what's going on, so we're flying in the dark."

Brody frowned at that. "I can go get a vehicle." He searched around behind them. "We're forty-five minutes from the house, and nothing else is even close to where we are right now."

"This is one of the more deserted roads. A couple properties are out here, but nobody I know," Legend offered.

Brody nodded. "I can certainly steal a vehicle to get us out of here. What I don't want is to set off any police alarms for a theft."

"No, we can't have that." Blair looked around. "Not exactly a place where we can hitch a ride or can call for help around here."

"No." At that, Legend continued to study his phone, as he sent off a second message. When his phone rang, he answered it quickly. "Right. No, that's not good news, but thanks." He turned to face the others. "The vehicle coming our way was found in a ditch about three miles from here, not very far from the time period that it should have picked us up. It should have been here five minutes ago, waiting for us, but it's pointed in the opposite direction."

"So, the bad guys were expecting it?" Blair asked.

"Or somebody found it and decided to deal with it in the process."

"What are you not telling me?" Larry asked, staring up at him. Blair put a hand on his shoulder and squeezed gently. "I presume the driver's deceased?" Larry asked.

Legend nodded quickly. "If Father never told you how serious this could be right now, that event should prove it."

At that, Larry slowly sagged to the ground. "All of this, just to … to keep me alive?"

"Not to keep you alive but to pressure your father," Clary explained. "If they caught you, they would use you to get your father to do what they want."

He looked up at her, and tears pooled in the corner of his eyes, almost on the verge of spilling over. "You know that's not what I want," he whispered.

"We know that, and we also know that it has nothing to do with you. These are adult games that should never get played, yet are played out across the world all the time," Legend stated, squatting in front of him. "We will deal with this."

Larry nodded. "Sure you will," he groused. Then he stopped, shook his head, and reached out a hand, palm up. "I know you will, but I'm getting tired," he admitted.

"Of course you are. We've walked at a fair clip, and you're carrying a good-size bag," Legend noted, motioning at the bag. "Take it off and rest while you can."

Blair stepped forward and handed him a granola bar. "Munch on this."

He snatched it from her hand. "You've got food?" He ripped it open, eyeing her with interest.

She chuckled and pulled out black licorice. "I've got some food, at least enough to get us forward for another mile or two."

"Good," Larry said. "I hate to say it, but is the car drivable?"

Legend nodded. "It will be coming our way soon."

"Was the driver killed in it?" Larry asked.

"No, he was dragged out and shot on the road."

"What about forensics?" Brody asked.

Legend shrugged. "What can I say? They'll find the body on the side of the road, and nobody will really have any idea."

"*Right*," Brody replied. "Secret service?"

"Definitely one of the good guys," Legend muttered. "Believe me. I'm not feeling very happy about his death either."

"Of course not," Blair added. Then she turned, looked around. "I hear something."

He frowned at her, startled—since he didn't hear it first—then checked his phone and nodded. "Sounds like the vehicle is coming toward us."

As it was, the vehicle glided to a stop not very far from them.

"There's no driver," Blair pointed out.

"No, there isn't," Legend agreed, "not at this point. We didn't dare take a chance with a second one. I'll be back in a minute." They watched through the trees, as he approached the vehicle cautiously. When there was no sign of anybody, he used his phone to quickly shut down the engine. Again using his phone, all the doors opened, including the trunk, and Legend made a thorough check, underneath the tranny as well as under the hood and in the trunk. Then he let out a whistle.

Brody whispered, "Come on. It's clear. Let's go." Moving quickly, they raced through the trees, up onto the road, and everybody got into the car, with Larry in the middle of the back seat. Blair and Clary took either side of him, with the two men in the front seat. The vehicle very quickly started again and drove forward.

"So, this is an AGV?" Larry asked in awe.

"It is, but I've taken control for now," Legend said. "We will also switch up the plates."

"As soon as we get to civilization, we can do that," Brody murmured.

"I also need food," Larry cried out.

"You've got food," Blair reminded him, handing him licorice.

"This is hardly food," he argued. "I could use a couple burgers, or how about some fries? I mean, if we're having a road trip, let's make it a road trip."

Clary burst out laughing. "I forgot what fun you are. I saw a lot more of you as a sickly boy, not necessarily one who was happy to be out for an adventure."

"Well, that sickly boy lost a lot of years," Larry stated, with more of that adult seriousness than anybody expected. "Right now, any adventure sounds like a good thing."

Clary smiled at him. "Got it, yet, at the same time, it's so good to hear your happy voice. And we can get food as soon as we hit civilization too."

"And civilization isn't very far away. I mean, we used to send Jed out to get food for us all the time," Larry muttered, around the licorice.

"We won't choose any close towns," Legend shared. "We can't take the chance."

Larry sagged back. "Got it," he muttered.

Legend looked over at Brody. "Not sure what you can do, but if you can put up a shield or a guard or sensors or anything …"

At that, Larry leaned forward. "What was that?"

"I was just asking Brody about guarding the car," Legend replied cautiously.

Larry gave him an odd look. "Didn't sound like that."

"Well, that's what it was," Legend snapped. He drove in silence for the next bit.

"And honestly, coffee sounds like a great idea," Clary added cheerfully.

Larry smiled at her. "So does pop."

"Pop is bad for you," Blair replied.

He sighed. "You're really such a downer sometimes."

"Yeah, well, it's all the joys of being the one who has to help you follow the rules."

"Rules are meant to be broken," Larry declared.

"That's what got your father in trouble," Blair noted.

With a sigh, Larry quieted and sat back. "There is that, too," he said sadly.

She winced. Legend looked at her through the rearview mirror, and she shrugged. "Sorry about that," she apologized to him. "I didn't mean to bring up any reminders."

"There will be lots of reminders," Legend said. "We can't get away from it, not with the situation we're in now. So, all of us are better off understanding that this is the result of our father's actions, and the sooner we get over it and figure out how to get clear of it, the better."

CHAPTER 4

B LAIR WATCHED AS the next town came into view, and Legend pulled into a gas station, where he quickly filled up the tank. "So, it's not electric?" she asked him, as she stepped out.

"It's a hybrid." He looked down at the sleeping Larry. "How's he doing?"

"Better than expected," Blair stated. "His resilience always amazes me."

Legend nodded at that. "Something is very unique about him. When he was born, I wanted to hate him—and hated myself for wanting to hate a child, so innocent and completely unaware of what was going on around him—but I couldn't even do that." He shook his head and laughed. "Larry was just too sweet. Too sweet, too good, almost too angelic for the world that we're in," he murmured. "Ever since then, well, I've kind of been an unwilling guardian."

At that he got a hard look from Brody. Legend stared back. "What's your problem?"

"Just your choice of terminology," he replied.

"Why?" Legend asked.

Such honest confusion filled his voice that Blair turned to Brody and asked him, "The word *guardian* upset you?"

He smiled. "It didn't upset me."

But she caught something between him and Clary. "It's

a term that you actually can relate to, I see."

Brody shrugged. "We can relate to all kinds of terms. It doesn't really matter what they are."

"Ah," she murmured and let him off the hook with it. "I guess when it comes to this kind of stuff, there's just so much out there that we never really know who's on which side," Blair murmured.

At that, Legend nodded. "Even you, even now."

Blair frowned at him. "Even now?" she asked in surprise.

Once more Legend nodded. "I still don't really know who you are."

She pondered that and then shrugged. "Good point, and I don't really know who you are either. I know that you're important to Larry, that he talks about you incessantly, always with a certain reverence," she added in a teasing voice.

Legend groaned at that. "The last thing I need is hero worship."

"Don't worry. The last thing you'll get here is hero worship," she vowed. He glared at her, and she just laughed. "He's a good kid, but he's different. His way of looking at life, his philosophy, all of it is very unique for somebody his age. It's almost as if he's one of the Masters reborn." At that, she got a hard look from Legend again. She shrugged. "Maybe it's just everything he's been through. I don't know, but he has a fairly unique way of looking at life."

"He does, indeed," Clary confirmed. "And a lot of that is because of what he's been through."

At that, Blair looked over at her. "Did you …" Then she hesitated, not even sure what she wanted to ask.

"Did I what?" Clary asked, with a gentleness that made Blair even more uncomfortable.

"I don't know, just something about the work that you

did with him before."

"What about it?" she prodded carefully.

"Any chance that it affected him in some way?"

"Absolutely it affected him," Clary agreed, with a smile, "and hopefully in a good way."

Blair wasn't sure what to say to that, so she just nodded. "Still, it seems weird to think of him almost dying, yet look at him now."

"A lot went into keeping him alive," Brody added, "and, for that, we have Clary to thank."

Blair didn't say anything to that because what could she say? She still wasn't exactly sure what to believe, given all the stories. How much of it was real, and how much of it wasn't?

"Don't worry about it," Clary noted. "It was just important at the time to try and save him."

"A job?"

"Well, that's what it started out as, yes, doesn't it always?" she pointed out, giving Blair a wry look. "When you look after somebody at this level, whether they are your own child or not, it becomes a connection that you can't really walk away from."

"I know," Blair agreed, sliding a look over at her young charge. "It's one of the reasons why I do what I do."

At that, Clary seemed to understand, but Legend was the opposite.

"Why, because you can't have children of your own?"

Blair didn't bristle at his question, although she would have, maybe, in another scenario. "I've never tried, but I would imagine I can. I've not gotten to the point of even contemplating such a thing." Then she shook her head to step out of something like a trance. "He will need food when he wakes up."

"He can do without for a time," Legend said mildly.

She smiled. "Yes, absolutely, but regardless of the adult attitude and everything else going on in his head, remember that he's still a boy, and you will regret causing that young boy to come out. He may sound old at times, but that boy can throw a tantrum like you have never seen in an adult."

He laughed. "Yeah, you're right. He's still a boy, and he's still my brother." There was such genuine affection in his tone that she looked at Legend, surprised. He raised an eyebrow. "What? You think I'm just an asshole who storms through his life with bad news all the time?" He shook his head. "He's a good kid and doesn't deserve what my father dishes out, none of us do."

"That's very true," Blair agreed. "And there will always be people who take the brunt of others' actions."

Legend shrugged. "It is what it is, and I can't say that I care anymore."

She smiled. "And yet, when Larry needed somebody, you came running."

"He's not responsible for my father's actions," he stated.

"I'm glad to hear that. And he still needs food."

"Message received." He looked over at her. "When this is done, what will you do?"

"I have no idea. I don't even know if your father is still paying me or whether that's even been brought up."

Legend frowned at that. "When I talked to him last, he told me that he had a severance package for you."

Her heart clenched. "Ah, that would have been nice to know. I had no idea any of this was planned," she muttered, as she looked around. "I gather I'm being fired."

"I don't think that's the term. I just think it's more a case of he wanted to make sure you got paid."

"Versus not getting paid?" She shook her head at that. "I haven't heard anything. Wish I'd been told."

"I believe there may be some sort of notification for you in your email."

She nodded a little grimly. "Maybe. It's a good thing that I haven't spent any of my money for the last while, isn't it then?"

He stared at her. "You really didn't know, did you?"

"No, I sure didn't, but, hey, your father's been a surprise from day one."

"How long have you worked for him?"

"Four, five years, just after Clary," Blair replied.

"That'll be hard on Larry too," Legend muttered. "He's obviously very close to you."

"That's what happens, and then it's like being torn apart, when it's time to separate. Particularly when there's no time to adjust. Like now, finding out plans were made, and I wasn't included and losing my position to boot." She shook her head. "I suggest we don't bring it up with Larry right now. He's got enough to deal with."

"Agreed," Legend muttered. "As soon as we fill up here, we'll head into town and get some food. I'll take a look and see if I can connect with my father, see if he's got any plans or places we can use."

"You mean, like secret hideouts?"

"Yeah."

"But, if he has them, won't other people know about them?"

Legend pondered that. "Well, I'll see if I can connect with him still. I'm trying to avoid the news because of Larry."

"Got it. I can't say I really want him hearing what's going on out there either. I pretty well kept him off all media as much as I could, but current events are still an important part of learning."

"They are, but they're also dangerous, particularly for a young boy like him."

"Any dangers I should know about?" she asked.

Legend shrugged. "All of this is bad news. We're just trying to do what we can to keep him safe. But we don't know more than you."

"Well, it's all I'm trying to do too," she murmured, "but I guess that time is coming to an end." She tried hard to keep the dismal tone from her voice, but it wasn't working. She always got attached to her charges. She knew she shouldn't, but how did one not? And, in this case, they'd been through so much, and Larry was a hell of a good kid. Plus hearing about her layoff in this way, …well, it was an even bigger shock.

"Don't disappear on him right now," Legend muttered. "We'll see what we can do."

"There's nothing anybody can do," she replied, with a weak smile. "I knew this time was coming. I just wasn't expecting it right now."

He studied her features for a long moment, then nodded. "Try not to make any quick decisions."

"Yeah, and why not?" she challenged.

He laughed. "You really don't take orders well, do you?"

"No, I sure don't, and, if that was an order, I didn't receive it," she muttered.

"Got it," he said.

Just then Clary joined them outside the vehicle. "Are you two done quibbling?"

"Almost," Legend replied, as he checked the gas pump

racking up the bill. "As soon as we're done here, my thought was to make some phone calls, see where we're at, and get some food."

"Good idea," Clary noted. "As for phone calls, Brody and I have checked online to see where the world is at. It's gone to hell in a handbasket locally. The coup is underway, and it appears your father is in the middle of it," she shared, studying Legend carefully.

"Of course he is," he muttered. "And, no, I don't want anything to do with it. I didn't have anything to do with it, and, just for the record, it's not my thing."

"I get it. I'm just not sure what his expectation is in terms of his son, if and when he actually manages to overthrow the government."

At that, Legend frowned. "Meaning?"

"Meaning, is he expecting Larry to go into Parliament with him?"

"I have no idea." Legend swore. "I sure as hell didn't need that thought brought up."

"And yet it must be considered."

"Sure it does." He scrubbed his face. "Father would be selfish enough to do that."

"As Larry's father, he'll do whatever he thinks is best," she stated.

"No, that's not what's best for Larry, but my father will do it anyway because he thinks being a family man will look better to the public."

"Well, maybe it will. Is he …" Clary hesitated.

"What?" he asked her. "Just come out with it."

"Is he dangerous?"

"He's planning to overthrow the government. I'm sure many people think he's plenty dangerous. I didn't know his plans until they were underway, and he refused to listen to reason. Besides, I think everybody's dangerous in the right circumstances."

"Will he get away with this? A successful coup doesn't necessarily mean successful in the long-term."

"I really don't know. There is an awful lot of opposition, and he's not necessarily being the smartest about it."

"Of course not," she acknowledged, with half a smile. "When was a coup ever smart?"

He nodded. "Still, I had hoped and still hope that he keeps Larry out of it, at least until things stabilize." Just then his phone rang. He looked at it, swore again. "Speak of the devil." He looked back at the gas pump.

"Go," Clary urged.

Blair stepped to the still flowing fuel pump. "I'll take care of this. Go deal with him." And, with that, Legend took several steps away and answered his phone. She looked back at Clary. "How long are you involved in this?"

"What do you mean?" Clary asked, clearly more interested in what was going on with the phone call.

"According to what Legend just told me, his father has terminated my employment." She kept her voice low in case Larry woke up, but it was hard to hide her anger and distress.

At that announcement, Clary stared at her in shock.

Blair nodded. "Not exactly the news I was really expecting right now."

"Yet ..."

"Yet it kind of makes sense, I know. Except, if I'm done, who is looking after Larry now—as in right this instant? Did his father even consider that? Wouldn't laying me off when the coup was over and the country stabilized be a better time for Larry? I'm the one constant in Larry's life. More so than his father. And he's not even here to take over. Still, the timing is a little awkward."

At that, Clary nodded. "I would very much like to ask you to stay on, but I don't have any means to do that," she muttered.

"Well, I'm not sure exactly when my severance package comes through," she added in a mocking tone. "I'm supposed to be getting some kind of communication from him, according to Legend. I presume it'll give me two weeks or something. At least I hope it does. But the termination is immediate."

"Any severance pay would be good," Clary muttered, the cloud on her face clearing. "Larry really loves you."

"Well, we've become quite close," she shared, "at least since you left."

"I had to leave in order to help others."

"I know. I get that," she said. "It's just such a fascinating look at life that you don't really think about it."

"No, I understand. Even I spent so much time looking after Larry that he will always be a big part of my life, and I know that you are one person who will understand that."

"Yeah, I sure do. It's odd, suddenly finding out that you're laid off, and look at where we're at." She waved her arms around. "I'm stuck here, wondering what I'm supposed to do now."

"I'm sorry," Clary said. "That's the last thing anybody needs right now."

"It's tough, but I'll survive. We just have to make sure that Larry's okay." Blair's voice broke a bit, as she turned and glanced back at her charge.

"Hopefully we can get him somewhere safe."

"I'm more concerned as to whether he'll be sent to join

his father in the capital, if and when this all goes well."

"It won't go well," Clary declared, and then she winced.

"Seriously?"

"Sorry, I don't have any reason to say that," she added instantly.

"No, but you know so much already that I don't know what I'm supposed to say to your comment, except that it's not good news."

"No, it's not good news," Clary agreed. "It's also something that I warned his father about, but he wouldn't listen. I keep coming back to the fact that I don't know if this stubbornness is more about his belief that a new leader is actually needed or the lure of the power grab."

"That's a hard one for any of us to decide, isn't it?" At that, Blair motioned toward Legend coming back. They turned to face Legend, as he strode across the parking area toward them, and he was glaring something furious. "So, not good news," Blair muttered.

"For my father, it's the usual. The coup is underway, regardless of what anybody else has to say. He's excited, thriving, in his element. He says it should be in the bag by tonight, and we're to find a place to lay low, until he calls for us later."

"And me?"

He looked at Blair apologetically. "He didn't really say anything about you, except that the status quo is to continue." She hated that relief washed through her at that because really it was just postponing the inevitable. "Well, I can certainly hang around for another day or two," she stated.

"He didn't actually come out and tell me that you were laid off, and, if you didn't get that email notice, maybe he never did send a severance."

"Well, I guess I'll find out, won't I?" she muttered.

He winced. "I'm really not happy that I'm the one who told you because maybe his plans changed."

"Maybe, but, if he thought about it then, it's something that he's probably still thinking about, and it's best that I know."

"That's not true. Right now he's not thinking about anything except us staying out of his way, keeping Larry safe, and him doing his thing."

And it didn't take much to contemplate how much danger doing his thing would be for the rest of them. "Did you tell him what happened?" Blair asked Legend.

"I did. He swore, told me to take care of it, and that he'd stay in touch."

Clary nodded. "That sounds like the man I know," she murmured. She turned and looked down at Larry, who was still sleeping. "He sleeps with the innocence of a child."

"Of course." Legend sighed. "In the meantime, good government men, thinking that they are defending their own leader, are dying right now," he said, his voice harsh. "And, once again, my father is right in the middle of it."

"What if he doesn't make it through?" Clary asked. "Has he made any provisions for Larry?"

"I have no idea," Legend admitted in frustration, as he faced her. "Defeat is not exactly in my father's vocabulary."

"I get that, as a leader, as an invader or conqueror, you know, it's an all-or-nothing thing, but, in his position, he's got a young boy to look after. And what happens ..." Clary stopped. "I guess there's no answer for what happens."

"No, but he is my brother, so I will make sure he's okay."

"I'm glad to hear that," Clary noted cheerfully, as she

got back into the vehicle. "In that case you might want to start thinking about food because he'll wake up soon."

He peered into the back. "No way, he's sound asleep."

She looked up at him. "Sure, for the moment, but he'll be awake"—she thought about it—"in five minutes, I would say?" She looked over at Blair. "What do you think?"

"Possibly less," she added cheerfully.

Legend groaned, looked at the two of them. "And now you two are colluding against me?"

"No collusion required," Clary noted, with a laughing smile. "We just know what this boy is like."

"Right." Legend stared down at Larry wistfully. "You've actually had more time with him recently than I have."

"We also worked with him a lot more when he was sick." Clary smiled at him. "That may not have been something you could do anything about."

"Sometimes I wonder." He eyed her curiously. "Sometimes I wonder just how much you did. Nobody ever talks to me about it."

"No, I don't talk to anybody about a lot of it," Clary admitted. "Maybe when this is over, if you have some questions, I can answer them. In the meantime, I'm all about keeping Larry safe so he gets a future, even if nobody else around your father does."

IT HIT LEGEND on the hard side to realize that, if something happened to his father, which was entirely possible given this nightmare, Legend's brother could end up as an orphan. Not something anybody wanted to think about. Something was so special about Larry, even though Legend didn't know what that was. He recognized that the others were all trying to protect Larry—beyond him being an innocent child. The more time Legend spent time with his little brother, the more Legend understood that the boy had a special grasp on life, a unique outlook, and that, if he was ever to do anything in terms of the world or on a global level, Larry needed to survive. Thus surviving right now was something Legend had been tasked with making sure his brother did.

For himself, Legend had been raised without his father, and maybe that had been for the best. Maybe even after a lifetime of wishing he had had his father in his life, it was a good thing it hadn't happened. It was one of those things you could just never know, until now as an adult, when Legend looked around and realized what a shitty situation *living with Father* was, and, getting the short end of the stick, Larry could end up alone in all this.

Not with Legend here, however.

With everybody packed up in the vehicle, Larry rose right on time, unfortunately confirming that these women knew a whole lot more about this child than Legend did. They headed into town, and, once they passed a couple of fast-food chains, Larry was wide awake, pointing out each one they could stop at. But Legend hadn't managed to stay alive himself all this time by making foolish decisions, and he only stopped when he came to one that felt right.

Soon he pulled into the back of a promising spot, or at least one not so risky. He spoke to the passengers in the back seat. "Stay here while Brody and I check this out first." After all three nodded, Legend and Brody exited the vehicle.

They regrouped not too far from the others. Legend looked over at Brody. "Food?" Legend asked.

Brody nodded. "Sounds good. Any particular concerns?"

"All of it," Legend snapped. "I don't like anything about this. The fact that we've already had the one vehicle taken out is huge. The fact that my father has actually gone ahead, and the coup is underway, means that anything and everything will be up for grabs as far as people are concerned, and that's not good. Someone will be looking to grab the kid to use as leverage. The bottom line is, I don't want my brother involved in anything to do with my father on either side of any of his dealings, at this point."

At that, Brody nodded. "You won't get any argument out of me. Besides, we'd have the women to deal with if we let anything happen to Larry."

Legend let out a bark of laughter at that. "Isn't that the truth? Somehow my brother has managed to get some pretty powerful champions."

"You're not kidding, and you really don't know the half of it when it comes to the champions on his side. The minute Clary got involved, everything changed."

"Well, I'd really like to find out the details, so I can understand in what way and how, when this is all over with."

"In that case, maybe you want to consider Terkel's offer."

"I'm still struggling to believe that you guys are private."

"We're private because our own government tried to blow us up."

At that news, Legend stared at him in shock. "What?"

"We don't really have time for it right now—particularly since we won't be here long for food, then have to move on—but believe me when I tell you, it got ugly. And this is our solution—coming out the other side."

"Did you need a solution?"

"Well, the problem remains," Brody explained, with half

a smile. "What do people like us do if we don't have each other? This is a very unique opportunity to stay together as a team with Terk, and our abilities are growing constantly."

Legend shot him another hard look. "Are you serious? Growing?"

"Very seriously." Brody nodded. "Yours will too, if you join us."

"I don't know. I'm not sure I'm up for it."

"Well, you'll have to make that decision at some point in time, but it's definitely not today."

"Why? What happens if I don't make the decision you want? You'll kill me?"

Brody looked at him and laughed. "Don't have to. By the time you've done this job, and you realize what it's like to work with people who are the same as you, you'll be begging for the job."

"Yeah, I doubt it," Legend replied, with a laugh.

"Or maybe, when you realize just how much that woman can do and how much she means to you, you'll be looking to do more."

Startled, Legend looked back to where Blair was helping Larry out of the vehicle. "What Blair can do?" he repeated, clearly bewildered.

"Yeah. I'm not exactly sure what she's doing, but believe me. She's got some serious energy power. It's all protective, and it's all good, wrapped and bound up in keeping Larry safe."

"Well, maybe my father wasn't such a fool to hire her then." Legend continued to stare at her.

"I can feel the waves of power coming off her, but she seems very unaware. Clary would probably agree with that, but you know? Once awareness sets in, she becomes a very powerful engine all on her own. Make sure when that ride comes along, you're on it."

Legend laughed. "Not likely. That's like mixing oil and water, and it doesn't sound like a great combination to me."

"When it happens, you won't know what hit you."

Legend shook his head, frowning at him.

Brody nodded. "I know firsthand because that's exactly what happened to Clary and me. We're as well matched as I could ever have thought possible, and the connection is way deeper than emotional." He hesitated. "It's …" He shrugged as he lacked a lack of word for it. "I know it'll sound foolish, but we're aligned on an energy level, two of the same frequency. The stuff we can do together and the stuff we can do with the team are all freaking unbelievable."

"Well, now you've got me intrigued," Legend admitted, "but I just can't deal with it now."

"No, you sure can't. Just keep it in mind."

"So what are you? An advance scout for Terkel now?" Legend asked, his laugh a bit nervous.

"If I thought it would work, I sure would. However, the bottom line is that you have to want something like this. It won't work any other way."

"No, that's true. I suppose it's not that easy to find guys like us, is it?"

"Not only is it not easy, it's downright impossible. Then, when you guys do show up, you're all ornery, cranky, and contentious."

At that Legend burst out laughing, as he followed the women into the restaurant. "You mean, just like you?"

Brody shot him a look. "Yeah, and I'm sure Clary would agree."

Clary tapped him on the shoulder and nodded. "Clary

definitely agrees, but right now? Both of you shut your energy down. I know you've got it out there searching for energy and danger, but, in this place, it's rebounding somehow, and it's starting to attract attention." And, with that, she gave them both a hard look and snapped, *"Now."*

Both men automatically shut down their energy, bringing their auras back in line.

As Legend looked around, he asked, "What is this place?"

"Well, it's the restaurant that you brought us to," she replied, with a note of humor. "What did you think you were doing?"

"I'm not sure, but damn. I mean, as far as places go, it's very powerful."

"It is. This place was built on a forgotten graveyard a long time ago," she murmured. "I can feel the spirits still moving."

He shuddered at that. "Why do people do shit like that?" Legend asked, looking around. "Don't they know that those people can get up and walk?"

At that, she burst out laughing. "Well, sometimes they do it just for that reason. Yet, in their world, that's not what people are doing."

"Well, then they're just not being aware enough," Legend said, "because damn. That's definitely what they're doing." At that, he walked in, smiling to see his brother bouncing about Blair, asking questions of life the whole way. "He's definitely got a full spirit, doesn't he?"

"He's got a very happy-go-lucky spirit," Clary confirmed. "He's also got a very strong healing spirit, and that in itself causes trouble." Legend shot her a frown. She shrugged. "I did what I could to shut it down, but there's only so much

I can do when you have somebody as pure as he is. People will be attracted to it—but not for the right reasons."

Legend groaned. "Don't tell me that my brother himself will be the reason that we end up in trouble."

She smiled. "Well, hopefully, with all of us here, we'll manage to keep him out of it, but I would definitely be alert for any trouble coming our way because of him. I don't know how much anybody actually knows about his energy or about what he's like as a child, or whether they're calling him, you know, *special*, but he is special in ways that nobody can even account for."

"Did you make him that way?" he asked, staring at her.

"*Make* him that way?" She shook her head. "No, I didn't *make* him that way, but I might have helped bring it out. I might have unlocked something. ... Only time will tell."

CHAPTER 5

B LAIR STRAIGHTENED IN her chair, a tingling sensation running along the back of her neck. She quickly glanced over at Legend to see a frown on his face and his gaze darting around the room. She got the message and looked over at Larry. "Hurry up and eat. We have to run."

He nodded, popped the last of his hamburger in his mouth, and picked up a handful of fries. Pushing his chair back, he announced, "I'm ready to go."

She laughed. "Well, at least let's grab a napkin or something for that." She pointed out the ketchup on his chin. As it was, a waitress came by with a small takeout container, and they quickly loaded up the remnants of everybody's leftovers for Larry to munch on in the car. Then, paying the bill, Legend added several bottles of water and rushed everybody out to the vehicle.

As Blair was last to get in, she looked at him and asked, "What was that?"

"I'm not sure," he admitted, his voice low, "but somebody was definitely watching us." As he got into the vehicle, his phone rang. He looked down to check, but instead of a call, a text came through. "Change of plans, everyone. We're switching vehicles. Get ready to transfer in about two minutes."

At that, Larry gave him a big fat grin. "Well, I hope it's

something decent. It's a little squishy back here." The two women stared at him. "Hey, look. I'm used to having my own space. You know? Where I can stretch out and sleep."

"Well, you might," Blair noted, "but don't expect it next time." Within seconds of the words falling from her lips, a vehicle pulled up beside them, and all the doors immediately opened up. On Legend's cue, they quickly scrambled into the large SUV. As he walked around to the driver's side, she saw him talking with somebody. She leaned forward and took a closer look but didn't recognize the new arrival.

Brody stepped out, clearly startled. "Riff?"

Riff lifted a hand and then, without a word, quickly disappeared into the shadows.

Blair leaned forward and asked, "Who was that?"

"That was Riff," Brody said, his tone odd, as they drove out of the parking lot.

"Friend or foe?" she demanded.

He laughed. "Yeah, we're all still trying to figure that out."

She stared at him in shock. "Please tell me that was a poor attempt at a joke."

"Oh, it's definitely not a joking matter, and I didn't mean it that way," he apologized. "Riff definitely would be considered friend more than foe, but he is definitely … different."

"Different, *huh*. Did he even say anything to you?"

"Yeah, he told me to be careful."

She nodded. "Well, I guess it could be worse."

"What could be worse?" he asked, looking at her.

"He could have mentioned we have somebody on our back."

"Well, we do, and we all know it, including you."

She shrugged. "Yes, I know. It would be nice if we had a safe place to go."

"That's coming eventually too," Brody replied. He looked over at Legend. "Unless you have a bolt-hole."

"I have a place I was thinking of heading to. Is it the best place? That I can't answer, but it is a place."

"Well, we can head in that direction and go from there," Brody suggested. "This was hardly part of our mandate."

"Yet, wasn't it though, really?" Clary asked. "My concern was getting Larry out of here, safe and sound."

"I'm out now," Larry piped up, "so how about a nice hotel?"

"Or, maybe not, maybe camping or something equally uncomfortable," Clary noted in a dry tone.

He glared at her. "Hey, I'm up for some interesting experiences, but I haven't really roughed it much."

"But you're always talking about wanting to go camping."

He nodded solemnly. "I just wonder how your version of camping compares to mine."

She laughed. "Right now, you don't want anybody to know who your father is or what your father is involved in," she explained quietly, "so the least like what you had before is the best choice."

"Right." Larry nodded. "There's always that reminder, isn't there?"

"Yes, at this point in time there must be." She smiled at him. "Plus, you're hardly suffering."

"No, I have a full belly, something to snack on, and a little more leg room, so it's all good."

"In that case," Brody said, "I suggest we head as far away from civilization as possible."

"But we can't just hide away," Blair muttered. "I mean, unless you're planning on hiding away until this coup is over and see on whose side Mr. Kartal lands." At that, the discussion turned to the pros and cons of heading out to the middle of nowhere.

Finally Clary interrupted, "How about we just rent a cabin somewhere? In a place where nobody knows us and under an assumed name? We can spend a few days, while hopefully some things will get resolved, and we'll get to the bottom of it all."

"We also have to stop for groceries," Brody reminded her. "You might eat like a bird, but I sure don't."

At that, Legend snorted. "Neither do I, and, if we rent a cabin somewhere, does anybody have any ideas on where?"

"Maybe," Brody suggested, then he quickly gave Legend directions to another district. "What we don't know is whether they have any room for us."

"Maybe give a call ahead to see."

At that, Brody quickly got on the phone, and, within minutes, he shared, "Okay, they have one large cabin left. The prices aren't terribly low, but … who the hell's paying for all this anyway? Are we actually getting paid?"

"According to my instructions, yes," Clary replied, "but, if he'll be around to pay for it, is a question I don't know the answer to."

At that, Larry sighed.

She clapped her hand over her mouth. "Oh, Larry, I'm so sorry. I shouldn't have said that."

"It's fine. I get that my father has put himself in danger. Does everything always come back to money?" he asked in a small voice.

"At this point, it kind of does," Brody replied. "You

can't rent cabins for cookies."

"Well, that would be an interesting industry to start up then, wouldn't it?" Larry proposed, with a laugh, prompting a chuckle from everyone, as the awkward moment had passed.

Relieved, Brody turned and asked Clary, "Is there someone back at the base who could check on that? Celia maybe?"

"I'm on it," she replied, already sending a message on her phone. It took about half an hour before she got a response back. "Looks like we've actually already been paid for a large portion of it," she said, "or maybe all of it. I'll have to take a closer look at the accounting. It's kind of a lot of money."

"Well, it's kind of a lot of money for you, but that doesn't mean it's a lot of money, not considering the larger picture happening the whole time we're out on a job like this," Brody reminded her.

"Understood. Must consider the business angle."

"A lot of people are involved, a lot of expenses at this point," he murmured.

Legend looked over at him. "Are you guys doing okay for money since you've gone private?"

"We are, but we're still setting up as much as we possibly can. Some of those initial expenditures are huge, and it will be a long time before we realize any kind of return on it all."

"Got it." Legend glanced at him. "But do you even need men?"

"Well, I would cheerfully be home with Clary if we had more men, but, in this case, she is the driver behind the job, so it wouldn't matter here. But honestly people like Riff and you tend to not operate terribly well within the structure of a team, but we always need extra guys on short notice, so having a few more people will help, especially since the teams and the assignments tend to be fluid."

Legend laughed. "Well, that's one way to say it. I would think that most of us don't like authority at this point."

"No, but it's not even about authority really. It's about teamwork, about following team mandates, and about looking after the other part of your team, even if things are dicey," he murmured.

"Agreed," Legend replied. "I don't have a problem with teamwork. It's saved me more than a few times," he muttered.

"Will you go work for them, Legend?" Larry asked in an excited voice. "That would be so awesome if you did."

"Yeah? What would be so awesome about it?" he asked, looking at his half-brother in the mirror.

"I don't know. I just think whatever Clary does is pretty cool. So, if you could do something like that, it would be really sweet." Larry looked over at Clary. "Did you ever tell him what you do?"

"I sure didn't, Larry. I don't talk about it with most people. Remember?"

"No, of course not, and besides, it's kind of hard to describe, isn't it? I mean, you take on really sick people and help them get better." He shrugged, then frowned and looked worried. "That's not really what I think my brother can do though."

"You don't know everything about your brother," Clary noted, with a half smile in his direction. "I think you'll find he is very capable of doing all kinds of things."

"But not something like that," Larry disagreed immediately and with such conviction that she twisted to look at Larry.

Even Blair leaned closer. "Yeah, and why is that?" she asked him.

"Because I think you have to completely detach from everything around you and work on a very different level to do the kind of healing you do," Larry explained. "I know that Blair can do it, but I'm not so sure about my brother though. He's always been much more about action instead of sitting back and relaxing in place."

"Very true," Legend agreed from the front seat, stunned at what he heard from his little brother. "That doesn't mean I can't learn to do it though."

"Oh, I think you could learn to do it," Larry confirmed, his voice serious. "I just don't think you would particularly want to."

Legend burst out laughing at that. "Well, that may be true, but it's hardly our problem right now."

"I'm not so sure," Larry replied. "We've got a lot of problems. However, if some of these can be solved—as we figure out everybody's role on the team—it will be easier."

Blair looked over at Larry, and her lips twitched.

"You're looking at me like I'm a child again," he pointed out, with that self-important air of an almost adult who thinks he should be treated as such.

"You're very mature for your age," she stated. "However, there is still such a thing as life experience that's missing."

"Yeah, but every time I try to get life experience, you guys tell me it's not safe."

She laughed. "Depends on the life experience you're looking for." She chuckled. "Some things in life you do have to be older to experience."

He shrugged. "Whatever. Can I have those leftovers now?"

With a laugh, Clary handed over the container from lunch. "Have at it," she said, trying to suppress a smile.

With that, he dug into the fries and added, "I don't care where we go, but camping would be cool."

"It won't be camping so much as *cabining*," Blair clarified, concocting the word on the spot.

Larry rolled it around in his mouth, mouthed it, and nodded. "*Cabining*, I like it."

She smiled over at him. "You are so very easy to please."

"Sunshine, blue sky, and fresh air," he noted, making the switch to that very prophetic adult in a heartbeat. "You know that there's an awful lot to be said about the simplicity in that."

"There's an awful lot to be said about it, all right," Clary agreed. "It just doesn't always work out for everyone."

"No, of course not," he murmured. "I could never conceive of my dad sitting back and relaxing in life. He says that, if you're not doing something or building something, then you're a waste of space and air. That always bothered me because is that how he thought of my mother? Is that how he thought of Legend's mom? I mean, are we all only here to do something, to create something better? And who decides?"

Nobody spoke, and he continued. "I guess maybe we're wasting resources if we're not doing something like that," he added in a contemplative voice, "but it seemed very harsh to me."

"Your father would be one of very few people who would ever think along that line," Blair noted.

"He does believe that everybody has a job to do, and, if you didn't have a job to do, you were nothing," he pointed out.

"Yes, I know," Blair shared, "because I've been on the

backside of his thought processes a few times looking after you. Although he needed me to do that job, it has changed as you've gotten older. Somehow, to him, it degenerated into it being not much of a job in his mind, so I wasn't much of a person."

At that, Clary looked over at Blair in surprise.

She shrugged. "He has an unusual outlook on people in life."

"I don't think I've ever had a conversation like that with him," Clary mentioned to the group.

"No, and, unless you actually had a specific purpose or reason for that to come up with him, it wouldn't be something he would ever bring up. But I have had some insufferable discussions with him, particularly over Larry here. His father has very strict rules about our purposes in life, and, if you're not trying to be somebody better, if you're not trying to do something big, then you're nobody. Basically, if you're nobody, you're wasting his time. And, if you're wasting his time, you're wasting everybody's time. Sometimes he would go so far to say that wasting oxygen should be a crime because you should be out there doing something with your life. If not for humanity, it should be for the economy." She laughed. "There was a whole lot more to it, and maybe I'm not presenting it all correctly, but he had very strict ideas about it."

"Wow," Legend muttered. "I don't think I've ever had that kind of conversation with him either."

"I think he was trying to put Blair in her place," Larry explained. "I had made a comment about how I wanted her to stay around, but Dad felt like somebody who was only looking after me was more like a mother role. So, since Blair wasn't my mother, she couldn't be in that role. Therefore, if she had nothing else to offer outside of babysitting or tutoring services, to him, she didn't have any value."

"Ouch," Legend said. He looked at Blair through the rearview mirror. "Is that right?"

"Somewhat," she agreed, with a crooked smile. "I said, he had very distinct views on the value of individual humans, based on what you did and did not do in life. Clary was in the clear because she had a very special healing gift that made her one of those who were valuable to him in the sense that it kept his son alive. But, for me, as a babysitter, even though I was effectively his teacher, tutor, and surrogate mother, among other roles, it wasn't good enough. It wasn't a role that he could accept as having enough value, outside of the fact that he needed my services for the time being."

At that, Larry gripped her fingers and said, "He might not have, but I would be lost without you."

She leaned over and kissed him on the cheek. "It's been a great ride," she murmured.

"Is it over?" Larry asked, with the suddenness of that adult inside a child's body.

"Well, apparently I'm to be laid off at some point along the line here. So soon enough, it will be, yes." At that, Larry sank back, just staring at her. "I'm sure it's a direct outcome of this mess we're in right now," she explained, "but, if you think I'll just jump out and leave you, you're wrong."

He nodded. "No, you wouldn't do that." He studied her, as if he knew more than she did. "Is my father really expecting that this will go so well that I can join him?" he asked, with such detached curiosity that everybody wondered what he could possibly be thinking.

"It's possible, yes," Legend answered. "You know he's always been extremely positive about any potential outcome that he's involved in."

"Even though so many of them didn't go well?" Larry asked, now deep in thought.

"I don't know that it was so much that they didn't go well, as that he doesn't pursue small and reasonable goals," Legend noted carefully.

"Do you agree with what he's doing?" Larry challenged.

"Me? No, not at all," Legend declared. "I'm absolutely against it. This is a government voted in by the people. Is it a good government? Maybe not, but it's the government that they have. To overthrow the government in a coup like this, well, it feels wrong. It's the kind of thing that happens around the world all the time, but, for me, it doesn't feel like it's the way to go about making change."

Larry was quiet for a long moment, and then he agreed. "You're right."

"I'm right from my way of thinking," Legend clarified, "but I'm not trying to turn you against what he's doing or anything else. However, if what Father does puts people in danger, I'm not sure it has the value that he seems to think it has."

Larry added, "He always says, it's not about me or us, but it's about the greater good."

"The things that people do in the name of *the greater good*, all over the world," Blair pointed out in a quiet tone, "is often not what anybody else would consider for the greater good."

Larry turned to look at her. "Now that's the problem, isn't it?" he whispered. He leaned back, closed his eyes, and muttered, "I just want to think for a bit."

She didn't say anything but looked over at Clary with a raised eyebrow because Clary was staring at him, with a worried look on her face.

"You just take it easy, buddy," Clary said. "This situation is about adults making decisions that you didn't have any input into. Those decisions are not necessarily ones that you'll be happy with, or want to live with, but you haven't been given a choice. So, in this case, the best that you can do is try to relax and let things play out."

"Even if it kills my father?"

"Even if it kills your father," she stated, "because your father has made this decision, this choice. Although most of us tried to talk him out of it, he wouldn't listen. His mind was made up, and nothing any of us did would change it."

Larry gave her a long soul-searching look and whispered, "That's all very true, but it still doesn't mean I like it."

And, with that, he closed his eyes and went quiet.

LEGEND LISTENED TO the conversation in surprise. These were adult topics that he wouldn't have suspected his brother to be involved in, but Larry did have a very unique point of view. Legend wasn't so sure about the decision to rent a cabin; it seemed to him that they were essentially stepping out of life and hoping things would calm down in the government turmoil, and then they could bring his brother back home. But what if the coup didn't go the way that his father had hoped? Had he made any kind of arrangements for Larry after this?

With his brother now sleeping in the back seat, he looked over at Brody. "Do you know of any arrangements he may have made for the long-term?"

"I was actually just thinking about that, and I don't really have any answers."

"Right, and that's something we will have to figure out," Legend noted.

Brody shot him a look. "Instincts?"

"Yeah, I'm pretty sure it's already mostly over."

"Sorry about that."

"He's nothing if not hard-headed and always very directed toward power moves," Legend stated. "It's made it very difficult to be around him, particularly when, if you're not with him, he considers you against him, and we're so very different. He considers me weak because of it."

"Really?" Brody asked, frowning. "It's hardly weak to have ethics."

"It is if you are on the other side of life," Legend clarified. "That divide can get pretty steep and difficult, especially if it's not the kind of divide that Father wants to see. Most fathers expect to have certain disagreements with their sons as they grow up, but I always stuck to my guns, and he could never really twist me to his way of thinking."

"Was he even planning on overthrowing the government back then?"

"I think he's always been planning on taking power, and, if he couldn't do it legitimately, he would do it any way he could," Legend shared. "I fought to keep Larry out of his father's world when it became obvious that he was heading in that direction, insisting that he keep Larry out of it because he was too weak physically to handle the stress. Father did agree to a certain extent, but we had many battles about it."

"I'm glad you stood up and fought against the type of things he wanted."

"He expected Larry to stay in the same house and just be

a pawn. However, since he'd already planned to kidnap one of his competitor's children as a pawn himself, Dad noted it could happen in reverse."

"Jesus. Did he go through with it?"

"No, because I put the kibosh on it. Believe me, it was only one of the many fights we've had. He didn't see the point of wasting leverage like that, until I pointed out that his own son would become that same kind of leverage, and, with Larry's health issues, that kind of leverage would kill him."

"Did it bother him or did he really not give a damn?"

"I think in his own way he cares about Larry, more than he expected, and it's the only reason he backed off that time," Legend murmured. "It was definitely one of those lessons for me, a chance to clearly see who my father had become. It's one of the reasons I've only been there in Father's life in a peripheral way. I just couldn't stomach his politics and his methods of handling disputes. As far as I know, he hasn't actually crossed any of those major lines, but, if he had and I had known, I would have tossed him in jail myself in a heartbeat."

"Yet you didn't do anything about this coup, or did you?"

"He actually kept his plans from me until the very end, until it became about saving Larry more than anything. I'd heard on my own that somebody was coming to snatch Larry and to use him as a pawn. When I pressed Father, he finally told me what was happening, and that plans were already underway and couldn't be stopped and that it was my job to look after Larry."

"Forever and a day?"

"Apparently. Obviously he didn't seem to even care that

I was hardly the best option for Larry."

"You're his brother."

"Sure, but look at the work I do. It's hardly a safe haven for a child." At that, a phone rang in the back seat. He looked back and asked, "Whose phone is that?"

"It's mine," Blair replied and then answered it. Almost immediately she stared at the others. "Oh my God," she whispered. "Yes. No, I understand." When she got off the phone, she stared down at it, then quickly checked to see Larry still slumbered. She lifted her gaze to Legend. Shakily, she said, "That was your father's property manager. He's just received word that your father has been taken by the police."

At that, Legend swore under his breath. "Okay, do we know anything about what that means?"

"No, but he did mention that he's sending me a package via email. He didn't say it was severance or anything, just a package. He also mentioned he's sending you one as well."

"Well, that's great. I'm not exactly in a position to sit here and argue with it. I've got to drive."

"If you want to pull over and trade, I can drive," Brody offered.

"No, we're almost there, but we'll need to stop for groceries too."

"There's a small grocery store just before we get there. Plus, I know the cabins stock a small store but only for convenience items, like maybe milk or something."

"Right, so that'll be another no."

"A small town is up ahead. Let's go grab some groceries there and get to the cabin."

Legend nodded. "Then we can sit down and go through whatever's been sent." At that, he took a quick right and then a series of turns getting into town, where he found a good-size grocery store.

At that, Blair hopped out with Legend. She looked back at the other two. "Are you okay to stay here with Larry?"

Both of them nodded, and the other two walked into the store. She grabbed a cart and started filling it with fresh fruits and vegetables. "Any idea how many days we're talking?" she asked in a low voice.

"No, plus we have no idea what will be in these damn email packages."

"I know, but, if anybody is out trying to find Larry, that's a whole different story."

"The problem is, if somebody decides that they need some leverage against my father, then my brother makes the cut. And, if they decide my father needs to be completely annihilated, then my brother will go too."

"Did you ever think that you might be on the leverage list as well?"

He frowned at first, then shrugged. "I wouldn't be surprised if my father had more than half-a-dozen bastard children somewhere. I know that he's acknowledged me, though not necessarily publicly. Larry is his only legitimate son."

"Right, so you're hoping that nobody else knows."

"Yes, that's exactly what I'm hoping, but honestly, I hadn't given it a thought. But now that you raised the point, it's a possibility that we'll need to consider as well."

She walked through the store, grabbed steaks, burgers, adding some hot dogs and other quick-cooking foods, then went to the cereals, sandwich goods, as well as bacon, eggs, and bread.

"Is there anything you want me to go grab from other sections?" Legend asked.

She shrugged. "If you can think of anything we need, just add it to the basket."

"I know we'll need coffee," he muttered.

"Good point," she agreed. "Grab some tea and hot chocolate too. I don't have anything for drinks yet." By the time they were done and heading to the check stand area, after the fastest trip that she could manage, the shopping cart was overloaded.

They checked out, restacking all the bags into the cart, and walked out to the car. She stopped and stared, nudging Legend, who was on his phone. "Where's the car?"

He raised his gaze and started swearing. "God damn it."

"Yeah."

Just then the vehicle came whipping forward in front of them, clearly driven from the shadows. Brody hopped out from the driver's side, and, moving quickly, put all the groceries in the back. "Jump in. We've got to go," he said, and, with that, they took off.

CHAPTER 6

BLAIR HATED TO say she was damn sick of being in this car, but she was damn sick of being in the car. They'd gone on a discombobulated ride around town, trying to shake off whoever had come into the grocery store parking lot looking for them. "Are you sure they were looking for us?" Blair asked.

Clary just nodded.

Then Blair looked over at Larry and frowned. "He's been sleeping for an awfully long time."

"I'm trying to keep him in that state," Clary admitted. "I don't want him to have any idea of what's going on. Not yet at least."

"Right, I'm surprised you could do that for so long. I mean, it's a helpful thing if you're a mother."

At that, Clary laughed. "Well, I'll be a mother soon enough."

Blair openly stared at Clary. "Are you pregnant?"

She smiled and nodded, gently patting her tummy. "Yes, my sister is too. We're twins, and we're both carrying twins."

"Wow," Blair muttered in shock. "On the other hand, you're so good with Larry, I'm sure you'll have an absolutely wonderful time."

"I don't know about that." Clary chuckled.

"I think we're pretty safe right now," Brody announced,

making another series of quick turns, sending them careening off to one side.

"That move doesn't feel like it's very safe." Blair gasped.

"Maybe not," he admitted, with a chuckle. "I just had to reroute us back onto our pathway."

"If you say so," Blair muttered. But, sure enough, within about fifteen minutes, they pulled through the open gate of a small resort, where Brody drove around to one of the cabins at the far end.

"Here is where we'll stay."

"If you say so," Blair replied, "but I, for one, am just very grateful to be getting out of this car."

"You and me both," Clary agreed, with feeling. At that, she gently nudged Larry. "Wake up, buddy."

He woke up, looked over at her with sleepy eyes, and asked, "Are we here?"

"We're here," she said, smiling.

He looked around, still rubbing the sleep out of his eyes. "Oh, wow. Look. It's on a lake." He sounded absolutely ecstatic.

Blair chuckled. "So, it meets with your approval then?" she asked in a teasing voice.

"Be hard for it not to. I've been wanting to go to a lake for a really long time. Can you teach me to swim?" He switched his gaze to his brother, then over to Brody. "Can somebody teach me to swim?"

"Sure," Legend agreed. "I didn't know you didn't know how."

"It's one of those things Dad didn't think I needed to know."

"Why is that?" he asked.

"He was never planning on taking me any place where I

would need it."

"Oh, right. I'd forgotten. He hates the water, doesn't he?"

"Absolutely," Larry noted in a cheerful voice. "But not me. I love it!" And, with that, he raced to the lake's edge.

"If you guys want to unpack, I'll go to the lake with him," Blair suggested, then took off after him.

"I'll come with you," Legend stated, immediately aligning with her.

She turned and looked at the other two, asking, "Are you okay if we do that?"

"Absolutely," Brody agreed. "Go keep an eye on Larry. We'll put away the groceries. As a matter of fact, we might even start cooking something."

Legend added, "Good. I bought stuff for hamburgers, hot dogs, and other choices, including some pasta."

"Good enough," Blair said cheerfully. And, with that, she raced behind Larry, who was already getting in the water. "You want to wait for me, Larry?" she cried out in exasperation but knew he was exuberant and full of life. She didn't want to do anything to hold him back when so much was going on in his world right now. He needed any moments of joy he could get. She laughed as he waited on the shallow end of the water, shoes and socks in his hands, with a big grin on his face.

"I love the feel of it," he exclaimed, as he turned around in circles until he fell, sitting down on the edge of the water. He laughed and laughed. "It's so beautiful," he murmured. "How could he not like the water?"

"A lot of people don't," Blair noted, "but generally it's related to a fear."

He looked up and nodded. "I think his mom drowned."

"Your grandmother?"

He nodded. "I think so."

"Well, that would explain it then," Blair replied. "However, that's not you. That's your father. You, on the other hand, get to start with a clean slate, and we'll begin with your lessons today."

"I don't have a swimsuit," he replied, looking up at her in horror.

"Surely we can find something that would work just as well. I would suggest shorts," she said, with a shrug. "That's what a lot of guys do." She looked over at Legend, hoping he would back her up, and Legend nodded.

"Shorts work just fine," he agreed.

At that, Larry beamed. "Can we start now? I really want to just dive in."

Legend shook his head, while chuckling. "Maybe for a minute. We'll spend some time here right now and then start your lessons in the morning. Everybody's pretty tired."

"Well, you guys are all tired. I'm not because I slept lots."

And Blair realized just how true that was. He had slept a lot. Just nobody else got any rest.

"Maybe we can go see what we can find to get changed into," she offered. "Then I'll come down with you."

"Promise?" Larry asked in excitement.

"Promise," she vowed, "but I also have some paperwork from your father that I have to deal with."

"Ooh, paperwork," he repeated, with a wave of his hand. "That always sounds ominous."

"Yeah, sometimes it's a little more ominous than other times. As soon as we get back up to the cabin, I'll take a look at that first."

He nodded. They stayed for another twenty minutes, maybe half an hour, and then Larry asked, "Is there any food?"

She laughed. "There is, but I don't know if it's ready to eat. Let's go up and take a look. You haven't even checked out the cabin yet."

And, with that, Larry raced ahead.

"Have you got any idea what's in the package that you got?" Legend asked her, as they walked slowly to the cabin.

"No, but I suspect it's my walking papers," she noted, "and that makes me feel terrible."

"Well, let's not borrow trouble until we get there," he said, then hesitated. "Did my father really think of you that way?"

"Absolutely. I never really made any attempt to dissuade him either though, so I'm not sure it's all his fault." Legend stared at her intently, and she shrugged. "Your father is pretty determined to see what he wants to see, and I never really saw him ever make an effort to bend or to give in, not in any way."

"No, it isn't really part of his makeup, is it?" Legend noted thoughtfully. "Even now, I know there's a good chance that he won't live to see tonight, and it just brings up all kinds of strange emotions."

"Well, he is your father," she stated.

"He is, but, once he went down this pathway, it could end only one way."

"Seriously? Did you always think this venture was such a lost cause?"

"Absolutely. I told him so, but he wasn't prepared to listen."

"So many times they aren't, are they?" Blair noted. "Anyway, let's go take a look at our respective paperwork, so we both have an understanding of where we're at. Then I'll have to make some decisions."

He nodded. "I was hoping that you wouldn't leave him right away."

"I wasn't planning on it," she said, "but I'm also a liability as long as I stay here." She faced him. "We're too many people to effectively hide."

"I was wondering about that too," Legend admitted, pushing his hair off his face. "We need a plan."

"Yeah, but we also need to know what the status is and whether your brother is actually in danger or if maybe this is over with and it's all okay now."

"And then what? As a young boy, Larry can hardly be expected to go back and live in that place all on his own." She didn't know what to say to that. By the time they reached the cabin, Clary was busy making hot chocolate for Larry.

Blair sat off to the side and quickly opened her laptop. Using the internet code, she brought up her email and downloaded the paperwork that had come in for her. When she opened it, she was surprised to see a missive from her employer. It was formal, telling her that she had been given three weeks of severance pay and that her employment had been terminated immediately. She sat back and stared at it. It's kind of what she had expected, even though she didn't really understand why he would do something like that in the middle of this turmoil.

Yet there it was in the email. As she read further, in the event of anything happening to him, he was attempting to separate from all known personnel in order to keep Larry safe. That made his firing of her a little more understandable, but what had he done in terms of keeping Larry safe? She looked over at Legend to see a look of shock on his face. "Obviously you weren't expecting whatever you got either."

Legend glanced over at Larry and then back at her, shook his head, and in a low voice asked, "What did you get?"

"My walking papers," she stated. "Apparently, in the event of things not going as planned, he would cut ties with everyone associated with him. I, of course, was part of that group."

Legend just stared at her and finally blinked. "Interesting tactic."

"Yeah, particularly since he didn't explain just what the plan was for Larry's care."

"No, of course not," Legend agreed, "but, if he'd asked, I would have said no."

"Asked what?"

"I've been given guardianship over him."

"Are you surprised?" she asked curiously. "You are his only living relative."

"Maybe, but generally you would ask somebody if you wanted to do something like that," he replied. "This is hardly what I would have expected out of my life at this point in time, and I definitely would have refused, at least to this extent. I do work, and all of my work is dangerous."

She pondered that. "What if you went to work with Terkel?"

"That's dangerous work too," he pointed out, "and I would still need a home base for Larry. I'd planned to make sure he was okay regardless, but this is a step further than I thought my father would go."

She nodded. "It's all a bit of a shock, isn't it? On the

other hand, Mr. Kartal knows how much you care about your little brother and trusts you to keep Larry safe."

"And for me? Well, look at the situation I'm in here. It's not as if I could just turn around and walk away from him and say, *Okay, I'm done.* I mean, we can't even get out of here safely."

Blair scrubbed her face and muttered, "I need to sleep on this."

"Yeah, you and me both," he replied in an odd tone.

She looked up at him. "Why? What are you thinking?"

He shrugged. "I don't know what I'm thinking, but, like you, I need to just let this settle for a bit." He got up and, in a sudden move, told Brody, "I need to head outside for a few minutes and clear my head." With that, ignoring Larry's call out to him, Legend quickly stepped outside.

Clary walked over, sat down beside Blair, and whispered, "What's going on?"

"Well, I've been fired—however you want to look at it," she shared in a low tone. "Effective immediately, with a three-week severance package, but basically told *Get out of our lives.* Apparently Legend's been given full guardianship." She kept her voice even lower so that Larry couldn't hear. "Without asking Legend first."

At that, Clary's gaze widened. "Interesting choice."

"His only living relative is probably the reason," Blair guessed, "but I don't really know. There was an explanation, saying that, should things go wrong over this, then he was cutting ties with everybody, and my termination is part of that, I imagine."

"That would make sense—probably everybody at the mansion as well. Yet, depending on how the coup goes, his properties could all be forfeited."

Blair nodded. "I just don't know what I'm supposed to do about any of this."

Clary studied her. "If you were still over there, and you received this, what would you be doing?"

"Arranging a way to leave," Blair replied, "not that I'm exactly sure where I'd go, maybe visit some family," she muttered. She wanted to cry, but this was no time for tears, and she didn't dare look at Larry. "It's the negative side effect of doing this kind of work, isn't it?" she asked after a moment.

"It absolutely is," Clary agreed. "We give everything of ourselves to our charges, so how is it we're supposed to not care when we look after somebody for as long as we have? It's an occupational hazard."

"Yes, and the fact of the matter is, now I'm to have zero to do with him. How do I tell him that? He won't necessarily understand."

"I think he'll understand, but it'll be the worst-case scenario for him because he's now losing you at the same time he's also losing his father."

"His father didn't seem to think that was an issue," she noted in a dry tone.

"It doesn't seem to me that his father thought beyond his own political agenda," Clary stated, with a harder tone than Blair was expecting.

She nodded and smiled. "Very true," she muttered. "Anyway, I'm pretty well out of it, and now I need to find a way to catch a lift somewhere and buy a ticket for someplace," she whispered, staring off in the distance.

"Where would that someplace be?"

"I'll go back to England, I guess," she replied. "I have family and friends I could visit, and then I'll have to figure out what I want to do next. I'm not even sure I want to do this work anymore," she said, looking down at her clenched fists. "It's ..." She just let her voice trail off.

"Traumatizing? That's the word I think of, but, if your charges weren't quite so cute and adorable, it might be easier to separate."

Blair laughed at that. "Larry's been special right from the beginning, as you well know, since you had a hand in it."

"Maybe," Clary murmured, "but I also had something absolutely wonderful to work with."

"Of course, and look at us now. We're all sitting here, doing our best to keep Larry alive and safe—mentally and physically—but apparently that job is no longer one I'm associated with." Blair knew she sounded *off* and odd. "Excuse me. I just need a few minutes."

She got up and stepped outside, then headed to the lake. She saw no sign of Legend anywhere, and she *was* feeling off. Yet that wasn't even the right word. She wasn't stunned because, to a certain extent, she'd known that this day would come, and, in the midst of this mess, it made even more sense that it would happen now. But she just hadn't allowed herself to think about what the repercussions would be, and now there was nothing else to be done but to deal with it.

She sat near the water for a long moment, her face buried in her arms. Hearing a sudden sound, she looked up, expecting to see Legend. Ready to give him a half smile, she was slammed in the head and knew no more.

LEGEND WALKED BACK into the cabin, sniffed the air, and asked, "Burgers?"

At that, Brody nodded. Clary came up and asked, "Can you go get Blair for dinner?"

He looked at her, surprised. "Sure. Where did she go?"

"Down to the lake. She was pretty upset."

He nodded. "Yeah, my father, in his usual smooth manner, completely surprised her."

"I think in some ways she was expecting it, yet wasn't truly prepared for what it really means."

"We're expecting all kinds of things, but it's a shock when it actually happens," Legend stated. "I'll go talk to her and bring her back for a meal." At that, he turned and walked back out of the cabin.

Lifting a hand against the bright sunshine, he looked for the best pathway that she may have taken. Not seeing much, he headed toward the lake, where they'd been with Larry. As soon as he got down there, he saw her footprints and where she'd been sitting but saw no sign of her now. He wandered up and down, but he saw nothing, except for multiple prints. As soon as he determined a second set was from heavy work boots, he froze, turned on his senses, and studied the energy around him.

Definitely hunters, definitely somebody was here. Now the question is, where is she? He quickly searched the beach areas, then headed to the tree line. When he couldn't find anything, he quickly raced back to the cabin, catching sight of Brody outside on the deck. Legend gave a sharp whistle, and Brody spun and looked at him, so Legend motioned him over.

Brody raced down to join him. "What's the matter?"

"She's gone," Legend said. "Found tracks at the beach, heavy boots. You need to keep an eye on them here, just in case it's connected., and, given what we've been through so far, I don't see how it couldn't be."

"Go find her," Brody said urgently.

With that, Legend headed into the trees, searching. He followed the tracks into the wooded area, but, at that point in time, the signs were much harder to find. A broken branch, a tiny bit of thread, but he kept following it, grateful that the sun was starting to go down.

When he heard a noise up ahead, he slipped behind a tree and watched as a man stepped out from behind another tree and slipped across to stare at the cabin. The stranger then pulled out his phone, took several photos, and sent a text.

Swearing and wishing he'd nabbed him before he sent anything, Legend was on him in seconds. And, with a quick hard fist to his jaw, the stranger was down. Legend grabbed the guy's phone, checked the last text, and then quickly sent another. **I was mistaken.**

With that, Legend pocketed the guy's phone and tied up the stranger, leaving him wrapped around the tree. Then Legend backtracked, and there, off to the side in a lump, was Blair.

He quickly untied her, picked her up, and, gently cradling her in his arms, he raced to the cabin. As he burst in through the door, Clary exclaimed and came running. "I think he hit her over the head." Legend turned to Brody. "Did you find anything?"

He shook his head. "I've put up a guard, although you just punched a hole in it."

"I'll have to punch another one," he stated. "I've got the guy who attacked her tied up down there. I'll be back with him in a minute."

And, with that, Legend quickly returned to where he'd

left the attacker. He stepped into the area, only to find his prisoner gone. Swearing, he pulled out his phone, called Brody, and warned him, "Watch out. The guy is gone."

"What do you mean he's gone?" Brody snapped.

"I left him unconscious and tied up, so either he's not alone or he's got a very hard head and managed to get up and carry on, which I am sure is bull. I'll do a full search of the woods to confirm there's no vehicle or somebody else out here waiting."

With that, he disconnected and dove into the woods around him, looking for the attacker. It didn't take long to realize that whoever had been here was now gone. That also meant that Legend and the others must be on the move as well because this guy would just return, bringing backup, and soon the area would be teeming with bad guys. Legend didn't know what a *guard* meant as far as Brody was concerned, but Legend couldn't take the chance that some *guard* was all they needed.

He raced back to the cabin. As he burst in through the door, he came to a skittering stop at the sight of two men with guns. One was held against Brody, and one was held against Larry. "What the hell is this?" Legend bellowed.

"We're friends of your father's."

"If you were friends of my father, you sure as hell wouldn't be holding guns to people in this house."

"Well, sometimes you have to get a little bit inventive," said the one man, glaring at him. "Wait. ... Are you the one who hit me?"

"I have no idea what you're talking about. I was outside and thought I heard noises."

The guy looked at him suspiciously, then shook his head. "I'm thinking you're the one who hit me," he declared, turning the gun toward him.

"If that's the case, I would only have done it with cause. Were you the one who knocked out poor Blair here?" He looked down to see Blair staring up at him, her bottom lip trembling. He tried to give her a reassuring smile, but things were not the way he wanted them. "What are you guys doing here anyway?"

"Your father won't pay us."

"You mean Larry's father won't pay you," Legend stated, making the distinction clear. "I'm not sure what you expect from him though. He hasn't got much now."

"How do you know he won't pay you?" Clary asked in confusion.

"What happened to him?" Blair was shaken but recovering.

At that, the first man looked down at her. "He's been taken into custody, and he's been shot."

Larry's eyes widened, and he looked like he was about to cry.

Blair reached across and said, "It's okay, buddy."

He stared at her and squeezed her fingers. "I gather whatever he was doing didn't go the way he planned," he whispered.

The other man gave a short laugh. "No, it sure as hell didn't," he snapped. "And we need to get paid, so we can get the hell out of town."

"What's that got to do me?" Larry asked, staring at him. "I don't have any money."

"No, but your father did."

"But once they start investigating his life, they'll seize everything," he replied quietly. "I've got nothing."

"We need money to get out of here," the man repeated,

yelling now.

"Well then, you need to go see his property manager, if Dad owes you money," Larry declared, stating the facts. "I can't even sign checks, and I don't even know where the money is."

At that, the kidnapper looked at him suspiciously and then over at the adults. "Which one of you has guardianship?"

"None of us at the moment. His father obviously made sure of that," Legend snapped in disgust. "Did you really think a child would give you the money?"

They frowned at him. "Well, one of you cares about this child, so we'll make sure that whoever it is pays in order to keep him alive."

"You can get your money back from your dad," the other one pitched in, with a smile, pointing his gun at Larry.

"What makes you think that if anything happens to the father, that Larry will have any money?" Blair asked them. "If the government seizes everything, he'll have nothing, and he'll be the same as you."

"I'm sure his father has hidden away money for the kid's care somewhere along the line," the second man suggested.

Blair twisted and looked up at him. "Really? The man who you know so well? Do you really think he secured any money for his son's future? Or did he put it all into this losing venture?"

The man's eyes widened, as he stared at her. "You really do know him, don't you?"

"I've looked after his son for quite a few years," Blair shared quietly, "and it seems to me that his father is an all-or-nothing kind of guy, completely committed and certain of success at every turn. I highly doubt he set aside any money for Larry's care."

At that, the two men stared at each other, as if unsure what to do with that information. The first guy spoke up eventually. "Well, somebody here needs to fork out the money, so we can get somewhere safe. If the authorities find out that we're still alive, you can bet they'll be after us too."

"Did you do anything wrong?" Blair asked.

He stared at her. "Well, we were involved in the coup to overthrow the damn government. What do you think?" he snapped.

"I think you bet on the wrong horse," Blair replied, equally snappy.

He took steps toward her, his fist back, as if to hit her, but she stood up to confront him.

"Go ahead. Hit me. That's who you are, right? Somebody who uses force to take things, whether it belongs to you or not," she muttered. "So, as far as you're concerned, if you can beat me up to get two pennies off me, you'll do it."

"Do you have two pennies?"

"No, I don't," she declared. "I've been working as a nanny, so what do you think?" He winced at that. "And a nanny for *him* above all, so do you really think he was generous?"

"Hell no, he wasn't generous with us either. That's why we need something."

"We have a vehicle out there, but that's all I can tell you." Her voice was hoarse. "Nobody here has any money. Not the kind of money you're talking about."

"What kind of money do you have?" the second man asked suspiciously.

She pulled her pockets inside out and said, "Like ten bucks."

"God," he mumbled in shock, then turned and looked at his buddy. "Do you really think he would have left his son broke?"

"It wasn't so much that he left his son broke," Legend clarified. "I highly doubt he thought that far in the future or even considered the possibility of losing."

At that, the first man started to swear.

"On the other hand, there are properties and probably a lot of valuables inside," Blair noted. "So you might get something from there."

At that, the men stared at each other, as if wondering. "I don't know, man. I'm not about to start lifting silver and trying to find a pawn shop," he explained. "It has to be big money. Otherwise there's no point."

The other man agreed. "Well, we can always kidnap somebody," he suggested, looking back at them. "Which one of you has the most important family?"

"Larry, of course," Legend stated, "but we all know how that'll work out for you."

"Doesn't he have any other family?"

"No," Clary replied, "neither do we." She looked toward Brody.

"What about you?" the kidnapper asked, turning to Blair.

She shook her head. "I'm the nanny. I have no family. It's kind of a requirement for working for him. You probably don't have family either, not if you work for Mr. Kartal."

He stared at her and nodded. "I never thought of that, but you're right. Why is that?"

"Because, if we have no one, we're disposable."

"*Disposable.*" At that the first man sucked back his breath and then slowly nodded. "That son of a bitch. If he thought that far ahead, surely he would have thought about his son."

"Only if his father has money after this coup, and, even if his father's dead, Larry can't even access anything. He is a minor."

"Well, crap." The two men looked at each other and stepped back. "We'll have a little talk here, so you just keep to yourselves and don't do anything stupid."

Clary looked over at Brody, raising one eyebrow.

Legend wasn't exactly sure what that look meant, but he presumed it was something along the lines of *What will we do?*

CHAPTER 7

B LAIR STOOD, COMPLETELY ignoring the gunmen, and announced, "While you talk about it, I'll finish the burgers." They stared at her. As she walked into the kitchen, still visible to them in the same open front room, where she carried on with the food prep.

"You don't appear to be too bothered by anything," said one of the gunmen.

"Well, you've just basically told me that I don't have a job. If Larry's father's been picked up, then I have my own nightmare to deal with. I will not go hungry on top of it."

At that, the one guy snorted. "Everybody who works for him no longer has a job. Anybody who had any kind of dealings with him is now under suspicion, and anybody who had business plans with him is now out of luck," he stated flatly.

"I guess in some ways that is to be expected, given the type of plans he had," she noted quietly, as she finished slicing the tomatoes and vigorously pulled the lettuce leaves off the core, as she quickly finished the preparations for the burgers.

"What will you do with those?" the gunman asked, coming up behind her. "I want you to go sit down."

"What? And waste good food? No," she replied with finality. "Unless you're planning on shooting *all of us*," she said with emphasis, "people need to eat. We're all tired. We're fed up. I, for one, have a bad headache, thanks to one of you. Plus, now you've just dropped a bombshell that will have some pretty strong consequences for all of us." And, with that, she slapped the burgers together and put them on plates. "If you're expecting a burger, you need to tell me right now, so I can put on a few more."

The gunman glared at her, and she shrugged. "If you're not, that's even better because we don't really have that many." She kept on working, ignoring the armed men altogether.

Frustrated, he turned and moved away, leaving her alone in the kitchen area. As he walked off, she heard him mutter something about *the crazy broad.*

She shrugged. From his choice of words, he was probably British then too, just her luck. She may run into him again in England. Shaking her head, she wasn't so much upset about losing her job. It was all about losing the connection to Larry, and yet, as she'd already acknowledged, she knew her termination would be coming at some point.

She looked over at Larry to see him sitting rather frozen off to one side, beside Clary. She had her hand on him, and even Blair could see the energy flowing from one to the other. Clary was one of those people who would always be grateful to be here to try and help, and Blair was really grateful that Clary was here too. With Blair out of the picture, Larry would have a harder time coming up, but it was also not something that Clary could take on full-time, not with her married now, and pregnant with twins, and working for Terk too. Blair wasn't even sure that Legend could handle it either. Being a full-time parent wasn't the same as being a part-time parent. Having full responsibility for a child was a completely different situation.

She looked over at Legend. "What do you want on your burger?" He frowned at her. She snapped, "Hey, I'm eating. If anybody else wants to eat, then come over and grab one. I've got most of them made up, but there might be a few other things you want on yours."

Legend rose and came over, and the gunmen just kept an eye on him. "Interesting move on your part," he whispered.

"Well, my life's just been tossed into the gutter right now," she murmured, "so whatever. At least we can eat." She handed him a plate with two big burgers.

He looked at it appreciatively and smiled. "It'll be okay, you know?"

"Well, some of it will be," she said in exasperation. "The rest of it? Well, that remains to be seen."

"I'm sorry. My father was nothing if not very focused."

"He's always been intensely focused," she agreed quietly, "and I can't really blame the man for that. It's really all my fault for getting too attached to Larry. I knew it was happening, though I couldn't have really stopped it. It was a good thing for Larry at the time, but now? Well—"

"It's still a good thing for me," Larry bellowed, glaring at her. "Just because this has happened, it doesn't mean I want you to disappear."

"I know that," she said, softening her tone. "I'm not made of money though, and I have to work for a living, so …" She shrugged. "I don't even know how I can make it work."

"Well, let's not worry about it right now," Clary noted. "I think we have bigger problems." She tipped her head toward the two gunmen.

Blair snorted at that. "You think? These guys are looking

for a way to make money, just like I am. I don't have anything to offer them. I don't have two pennies to pull together myself," she muttered. Then she turned, looked at Brody and addressed him. "Brody, your turn. I've got two burgers here made up for you." She walked over and handed him the plate. He accepted it in surprise, looking over at the gunmen, staring, standing off to the side, just letting their captives eat.

Brody shrugged. "Good enough." Then he started munching away.

She looked at Legend to see the surprised look on his face and then his acceptance, as if to say this was a moment that they would take, and they would eat because they didn't know if they would get another moment to do so. She smiled at Clary. "Your turn," she said cheerfully.

Clary nodded and asked, "You want to come sit here with him?"

She nodded, then walked over to Larry, sat down, and put an arm around his shoulders. "Buck up," she told him. "You'll be fine." He looked up at her, and she saw the tears wanting to pour. "I promise. It will be okay."

"*Yeah?* You can't promise that. If my father's dead, everything in my world just flipped."

"That's quite possible," she agreed quietly, "and there will be people after you, as we well know. However, if you don't have any money, and you don't have anything to give them, maybe they won't feel the need to take you."

He gave her that look and replied, "You know that, in many ways, I've already overstayed my welcome in this world."

She froze, looked at him, and asked, "What do you mean by that?"

"Well, I wasn't supposed to live this long, so, if I die now, … well, I guess that's just the way the world rebalances itself."

She winced. "Don't even think like that," she snapped, glaring at him. "You have just as much right to a full and healthy life as anybody else."

He gave her a ghost of a smile. "You all can work as hard as you can to keep me alive, but you still can't make sure of it."

At that, one of the gunmen stepped over and asked, "What are you talking about?"

She sighed. "We almost lost Larry not all that long ago. He was very, very ill. He's still not back to full health, so this is definitely not helping him."

"Well, *so sorry*," he said in a mocking tone. "We're trying to figure out what to do."

"I get that, but it's not our problem—and certainly not Larry's," she snapped, "As far as I know, Mr. Kartal had money, but, if he's been taken, I don't know how it stands with his assets. The onsite property manager is a possibility. However, I doubt any cash remains or that it's negotiable."

"Who is the property manager?" the one guy asked.

She gave him the name. "But honestly I don't know if he can do anything like this or if he's just from an accounting firm in London."

At that, the guy winced. "With our luck that would be exactly what he's done," he muttered. "The bastard."

She stared at him. "So, did you just not get paid or were you supposed to get a portion out of the proceedings?"

"Both," he said. "Not that it'll help now."

She nodded and didn't say anything. Sometimes it's better to just cut and run. At that a phone rang. She looked around, startled to realize it was hers. She got up and walked over to the kitchen ledge where she had left it, but one of the gunmen snatched it from her hand.

"Who is it?" he snapped into the phone. When nobody answered on the other end, he turned and asked her, "What did you do?"

"I didn't do anything," she declared, staring at him. "What are you doing answering my phone? For all you know, it's my girlfriend."

He glared at her and asked, "Why didn't she answer?"

"Well, because no man should be answering my phone," she declared. "Now what you've done is alerted her that I could be in trouble, and she'll be worried."

He tossed the phone to her and stated, "Call her back and tell her everything is fine. Say convincingly that you're busy." When she hesitated, he pressed the gun against Larry's head.

Larry looked over at her, and she nodded. "If you harm Larry, I can guarantee that you will never get a dime." Not only was her tone terse and intimidating, but she stepped closer to the gunman, who backed up a step.

With that, Larry smirked, and the gunman lowered his gun.

She hit Redial on her phone, recognizing Terkel's number, and, before he could say anything, she told him, "I'm fine, baby. Everything's okay. I'm just really busy. I'll call you back when I have a chance." And, with that, she ended the call. She looked over at Brody to see an odd look on his face, one of concentration though, and she realized something was going on that she didn't understand.

But then they all seemed to have skills and abilities that she'd never seen before. Even as she looked over at Legend, she saw something odd on his face. as he looked at her. She smiled down at Larry. "It's okay, buddy. Just stay calm. It's okay."

He looked at her and smiled. "You always say that. You always make it sound like everything will be just fine."

"Because it is," she stated. "Besides, life is way too stressful to be worrying about it right now."

Larry gave a short, stuttered laugh. "There's nothing I can even do. My father is dead," he cried out, clearly in such pain that she immediately opened her arms and wrapped them around him, hugging him close.

"I know, kid. Even if he isn't yet, he will be soon," the gunman agreed, looking over at him. "Sorry, kid, but your dad bet on a particular pathway, and it wasn't any good."

Larry nodded. "If it had been good, would you still be standing here, holding a gun to my face?"

The gunman stared at him, then slowly shook his head. "No, because your dad would have paid me."

He nodded but winced. "Maybe he would have paid you," Larry noted sadly. "But you should know that he has history of not paying people."

At that, the gunman frowned. "How do you know that?"

"I've just heard things as people were yelling on the phone sometimes," he replied. "People get angry because they expected something and didn't get it."

At that, the gunman looked over at his buddy nervously. "Is that true?"

"I don't know," he muttered, staring at the kid. "Anything in particular?"

Larry shrugged. "Not really. He just seemed to always have angry people on the phone."

"Yeah, I wonder why," snapped one of the gunmen, "if

it's not paying people."

"Have you worked for him long?" Blair asked him.

The gunman turned his gaze back to her. "How come you didn't get a burger?"

"Because I came over here to comfort Larry," she said quietly, only half lying. She'd come over to let Clary go to the kitchen, away from them. Blair wasn't sure what was going on between her and Brody, but, with their hands together, they looked different. She asked Larry, "Do you want a burger?"

He shook his head. "No," he whispered. "I can't eat right now."

She nodded. "I get it," she muttered. "I'm so sorry."

He gave a shuddering nod and then said, "I would take an apple though."

She laughed. "An apple would be good." She got up, walked into the kitchen, where all the groceries were, and fished out an apple from one of the bags. She washed it and patted it dry and then brought it back to him. "Here. Crunch into that."

"What good will an apple do if he doesn't want to eat?" asked one of the gunmen, suspiciously looking at her.

"Well, he gets blood sugar issues, and sometimes, when his stress gets too bad, his jaw can lock up, so an apple helps him to destress." The gunman didn't quite know what to say to that, but then he apparently didn't know what to say where kids were concerned at all. She looked over at the others, hoping that they would come up with a plan pretty-damn soon because she was getting tired of this.

As she sat back down with Larry, he told her, "Go get yourself a burger. I'll have the apple."

She hesitated, then nodded. "I'll go grab one." She rose

and quickly snatched a burger, standing at the counter as she plowed into it. "Pretty good."

"How can you eat like that right now?" the gunman asked, staring at her curiously. "Most women would be far too upset."

"Maybe so," she murmured, "but sometimes life is hard, and you get caught up in all these dramas, and there is just no way out. I don't know what your plans are. You could be set on killing us, for all I know, but, if you take us anywhere, who knows when we'll get food again."

"I don't have any plans on killing you," the first gunman stated, "unless you give me a reason."

She eyed him and then slowly nodded. "Wasn't planning on it," she murmured.

"Good." He glared at her. "It's just weird that you're all sitting here, eating around us though."

"Hey, I offered you a burger," she pointed out. "Still a couple are over here, if you want one."

He stared at her, snorted, and walked away. "God, they're weird here."

And that seemed to be all he had to say about it. She looked back at the others to see Legend munching away on his burgers, studying the gunmen. When finished eating, he walked over and put his empty plate in the kitchen sink.

The gunman immediately turned, holding his gun at the ready.

Legend shrugged. "Hey, just returning my plate." And he stepped away.

At that, the gunman sighed. "I don't know why the hell you guys aren't at all panicked."

"I don't think panic will help much," Blair noted.

"It doesn't matter if it'll help much or not," the gunman

argued. "This is not normal behavior. It's as if you guys are waiting for something, although I don't know what the hell that could be, certainly not a rescue."

"No, of course not," Blair seemingly agreed. She turned, filled the sink with hot soapy water, and started doing the dishes. She figured the complete mundaneness of it all was driving that one kidnapper nuts. All Blair was doing was giving the others a chance to formulate some sort of a plan, but Blair needed them to do it faster because she was quickly running out of ideas. If they somehow thought she had a plan, well, she really didn't.

Then she stared down at the hot soapy water and looked over at the two gunmen. When one of them walked over to the window, she glanced back at Legend, who was studying the other gunman closely, but trying not to make it look like he was. She smiled at that, then looked at Brody to see him studying her.

She shrugged, picked up the bowl with the hot soapy water, then turned. In a smooth move, she flung it in the nearest gunman's face. He roared, but, even before he had a chance to do anything, Legend had tackled him, and Brody was on the other gunman. It was all over in a matter of seconds.

LEGEND LOOKED OVER at her. "Interesting timing."

She shrugged. "I was waiting for you guys to choose the time," she explained, "and, when that didn't seem to be happening, I figured that a distraction might help."

"It did. We were just trying to sort out who and what they were after," Brody added, as he tied up his unconscious gunman.

"Yeah?"

"Well, unless you guys want to open up that pathway of communication and fill me in, I'm on my own here," Blair told them. "I didn't have any idea what you were up to. I figured you were waiting for something, but I didn't know what that something was."

Legend laughed. "It's all good. Besides, it's the same result. We've got the gunmen, and now we can decide on what happens next."

"Yeah?" Blair asked. "So what do you want to do? Is the local government looking for these guys as part of the overthrow attempt?"

At that, Legend looked at her with respect and nodded. "That's not a bad idea."

Just then a phone rang.

"Terkel, yeah. I know. It's fine," Brody said, speaking into the phone. "We've got the gunmen under control. Thanks for the help by the way." He finished the call.

Blair looked over at him, one eyebrow raised. "Thanks for what help?"

He laughed. "I'll explain later, but just be assured that we weren't alone on this, and we were trying to figure out who these people were and whether they had others outside, before we took them down."

"Well, can't you do that now that they're unconscious?"

"There is only so much information we can get while interrogating them when they're unconscious," Brody quipped. "It's much better if they're awake because that's when they're actively thinking, and we can read their minds."

"Oh," Blair muttered, her heart sinking, as she stared at

him. "I didn't think of that."

Legend walked over, wrapped an arm around her shoulders, and said, "It doesn't matter. You did good."

"So, you knew about it too?" she asked Legend.

"I knew they were up to something, and I had a good idea just because of the odd look on Clary's face," he revealed, with a smile. "Not exactly sure what all they were up to, but that's a different story."

"As long as I didn't mess it up."

Hearing an odd sound, Legend turned to see Larry getting up, no longer frozen in place. Then, racing forward, he threw his arms around Blair in a big hug.

She held him close and whispered, "It's okay, buddy. I told you that it would be okay." He looked up at her, and she saw the tears in his eyes. "Pretty tough day for you."

"Is Dad dead, do you think?"

"I'm afraid he may be, yes," Blair replied, with a nod, "but again we'll have to wait for confirmation of that." She looked over at the others and saw it on their faces too. "I think all of us suspect he is, but ..." Blair shrugged. "You know as well as I do how that isn't necessarily the truth."

"It feels like Dad's dead," Larry announced suddenly.

"That's why I'm telling you what I think too," she murmured. "No point in us telling a lie. It feels very much like he's already gone."

JUST THEN LEGEND'S phone rang. He fished it out and checked the ID on the screen. "Jacoby, what's up? ... It is, is it? ... Fine," he murmured. "I haven't had a chance to get through too much of the paperwork yet. ... No, I am aware.

It would have been nice if he'd discussed it with me first." Legend's gaze went to his brother.

At that, Jacoby added, his voice somber, "There is money, and there is a little bit of time, but we'll have to move on this right now. It was always in his plans to provide for his boy, but I am still transferring all the property. We moved some of it before this happened, when he jumped up the time frame on me."

"Of course," Legend noted.

"Whatever there is, as soon as everything is secured in Larry's name, we'll sell it anyway," he explained. "Larry needs a new start." By the time they finished discussing the business side of things, and Legend ended the call, he turned to face his brother and then nodded. "Your father tried to escape. He felt sure he had the support of the military and that they would back him up, but it appears that wasn't true. Anyway, during the escape attempt, he was shot, and your father is dead."

Larry looked at him and stiffened. "He was your father too," he pointed out.

At that, Legend closed his eyes briefly and nodded. "*Our* father is now deceased."

Larry sniffled, looked up at Blair. "We were right, weren't we, just then?"

"Yes, we were. Remember that intuitive part? It's often right."

"I know. I just didn't want it to be right."

"Of course not," she whispered, hugging him close. "He was your father."

Larry nodded. "Now I just feel guilty."

"Why do you feel guilty?"

"Because the pressure is over," he replied. "That pressure

to be somebody I'm not, to always be something different from what I am because that's what Dad wanted. It was never what I wanted, and I could never be that person. Now that he's gone, I wish I was that person so he would have been proud of me, at least just a little."

"Oh, sweetie, your father was proud of you, just as you were—even when you proved to be smarter than him—and you have nothing to feel guilty about," she whispered and held him close.

Legend felt a muscle in his jaw twitch at Larry's words because Legend certainly understood the pressure to be something his father wanted. Despite what Blair just said, Legend had never managed to succeed in making his father proud of him. His father was just not one of those people who could ever give a compliment or even the time of day to somebody who was different than him. He despised those who had different beliefs and values. Legend and his father had come to blows more than a few times, but, when the end had actually come, his father had left him in charge of his son. Which could be seen as both a compliment, yet, at the same time, a huge challenge.

He gently ruffled Larry's hair. "We'll get through this, buddy." Larry turned and looked up at him, so Legend opened his arms and swung him around and just held him. Together, they walked over to the window, and the two of them just hung on to each other for a long moment, acknowledging that what had happened was something they had both known would occur. Both had tried to dissuade their father, but there was no stopping it. Not once their father had put things in motion.

"He wasn't easy," Larry whispered.

"No, he sure wasn't. Yet he was your father, and we'll

honor that."

"He was your father too, but you don't see him like that."

"I know. Sometimes it's easier to forget."

"Because you had a different mother?"

"My mother wasn't any happier," he shared. "I'm not sure our father had the ability to make anybody happy."

"I don't think he cared enough to try," Larry noted, with one of those adult comments that had startled Legend time and time again.

"Maybe not, but that doesn't mean we have to live that way any longer."

"What about the gunmen?"

"Somebody is coming to pick them up," Legend told him. "These men are part of the team who went to overthrow the government, so it's best if they're taken back to face justice."

"What if that means they'll get shot too?"

Legend faced his younger brother. "I get that, but they must face the consequences of their actions. Is this how you want them acting when going around the world if they're free instead of jailed? Kidnapping people, holding them hostage, and trying to get money?"

At that, Larry winced. "No. I definitely don't."

"If they're given a trial and a chance to defend themselves, that will be best for everyone, and you'll see it. However, right now? There is just so much heartache and pain for everybody involved in this whole mess."

As Legend laid Larry down to sleep quite a bit later, Legend stared at his little brother for a long moment, watching him doze. Blair came up behind him, gently patted him on the back, and whispered, "You'll make a great father."

"It's not a role I expected to play," he replied, his voice harsher than he wanted.

"No, and I get that. I'm just not sure we have a choice sometimes."

He looked over at her and smiled. "Even if I did have a choice, I'm still not sure I would have chosen fatherhood."

"Because of what you've seen in life?" she questioned.

"My father wasn't easy, and I always worried I would be too much like him."

"I don't think you can blame your father for that," she replied. "I think it's a common-enough problem with all men. They worry about being a good-enough father or that the influence of the terrible parental figures they had themselves would make them not good father material. However, I think mothers have the same problems. Some of us have terrible upbringings, and we wonder if we should ever be allowed to procreate—in case those same habits procreate as well," she muttered.

He considered her for a moment, then nodded. "That's the real reason you haven't pursued having a family, isn't it?"

"Well, it's not as if I have a herd sire," she added, with a pointed look. "At least not one who I cared to go in that direction with. Still, I didn't have a good upbringing, no."

"Any particular reason?"

"My mother was on drugs most of her life. It was always drugs or men, and most of the time it was both," she stated bluntly. "Not exactly a good way to raise a child. I was put into foster care when I was twelve, after she died of an overdose, and believe me. That wasn't any easier."

"I'm sorry. We never really know what somebody else is going through in life or what they've gone through in the past, do we?"

"Well, the fact that we even get to adulthood with our sanity is sometimes a miracle in itself."

He chuckled at that. "I won't argue with that because it makes far too much sense."

"The fact of the matter is that this is what you've been dealt with now," she stated, "and I'm not sure how you'll handle it." He ushered her back into the other room.

"After having one quick conversation with the lawyer handling my father's estate, it seems there is a certain amount of property. Some of it's being moved right now into Larry's name, and some of it is being seized. Whatever is retained will ultimately be sold, and the proceeds will go to Larry's care," Legend explained.

"Good, that will help, and he'll need that—although I think he needs a father figure far more than he needs money."

Legend laughed. "Honest to God, I hear that time and time again, about needing a father figure, and then you see what there is for a father, and you realize that maybe you didn't need that father figure after all."

"That goes back to the conversation we just had," she said, with a nod.

Legend asked, "I guess what I'm wondering is, if you're interested in still looking after him?"

She stared at him, then sank into a nearby chair.

"What I'm really asking is, do you want a job?" Legend added.

CHAPTER 8

"WELL, THAT'S NOT what I expected you to say." Blair stared at Legend, but, inside, her heart swelled at the opportunity being tossed her way. She wouldn't have to separate from Larry right away. It would help all three of them.

"And it's not a bad answer right now," Clary noted, joining in. "For stability alone, it would be a good idea. Larry can't keep losing people."

"Puts my life on hold," Legend noted.

"Puts my life on hold too," Blair stated, with a shrug. "I'm not sure what I want to do or where that would be. Now that I have the termination, and freedom in one way, I have to take another look at my life too." Then she stared in the direction where Larry was sleeping. "I could certainly do it on a temporary basis to help him get settled somewhere, somehow. I'm just not sure about long-term."

Legend nodded. "Well, if you could even do short-term," Legend replied, "I would appreciate it."

She sighed. "A couple months kind of short-term?"

"How about a year?" he offered. "Then we can reevaluate."

She glared at him. "How about we compromise at six months?"

He grinned. "I figure by then that Larry will have you

convinced that you need to stay."

"Listen. I'm not his mama," Blair stated, "so there is that to consider. If you get married or maybe settle down with someone at some point, having me in the midst of it wouldn't help Larry bond with someone new in your life."

Legend snorted. "Yeah, do you see anybody lining up for that job?"

At that, Brody burst out laughing, joining them for the moment. "Good luck with that. You know that there is an underlying thread here that I find absolutely hilarious."

Clary reached over and pinched her husband. He glared at her. "What was that for?" But she just shook her head at him and gave him a pointed look. He tucked her under him and continued. "Hey, we all went through this. I think it's only fair."

Blair looked at him in confusion.

Brody sighed, as he glanced at the couple before him, then spoke to his wife. "It will be much more fun when they understand."

"Yes," Clary agreed, "but they're not there yet."

"Maybe not," Brody concurred, "but, if she doesn't agree, they won't get there either."

At that, Blair glared at him. "What are you two talking about?"

Brody raised both hands in frustration. "Never mind. I'll go outside for a bit."

"You do that," Legend agreed, "and keep an eye out."

At that, Brody froze, then turned toward him. "What are you thinking?"

"I'm thinking that where there was one group, there could be others," he shared. "And, no, I don't know for sure that anybody will still be after the boy, but we can't be sure."

"Fine," Brody replied. "I'll do a reconnaissance mission and confirm it's all clear for the night at least."

"And then," Clary spoke up, "we'll have to have a talk about what to do next time because, as much as we might want to think it's over, I'm not convinced Larry is safe. Even if you guys think so, I'll stick around him for at least the next few days to ensure he holds up okay. I don't want him dropping out of life because it's become too hard."

At that, Blair gasped. "He wouldn't do that, would he?"

"He's really strong, much stronger than when he was younger, but his spirit is suffering right now," Clary explained. "As anybody would be who has just lost their one and only parent, but you also know how he feels about being a burden, and that'll play into this as well."

Blair winced and shook her head. "Yeah, we really didn't need that conversation to happen, but hopefully he didn't hear anything."

"It doesn't matter whether he heard or not, he'll know on an intuitive level."

At that, Blair wandered back to the bedroom to check on Larry and smiled reassuringly as he slept. She returned to the other room and nodded. "Six months for sure, and then we'll see," she declared, with a glance at Legend.

"Fine," Legend said. "I'll take it."

"Good," she muttered, then looked over at Clary. "What are you thinking? What does Larry need?"

Clary hesitated, then spoke. "Well, I would say that you guys might as well come back to our place, but I don't know what stage of reconstruction we have back at headquarters."

"Is it safe?" Blair asked.

Clary looked at Brody sideways. He shrugged and said, "Safer than most places." Again, Clary pinched him.

"Why would you want to do that? To bring us back if that's the case?" Blair asked them.

"Well, for one thing, I know that the team would like Legend to work for us, but we don't want to pressure him into it."

Legend snorted. "I'm not sure Terk even knows what I can and cannot do."

"Do *you* even know what you can and cannot do?" Clary asked. "I've seen an awful lot of energy emanating from you. For example, that much crazier drive when Brody was at the wheel than when you were driving because you were cloaking the car, weren't you?"

He frowned. "Did you notice that?"

"I didn't notice it until Brody was driving and realized that he couldn't cloak the vehicle. Yet, because you weren't driving, you weren't looking after it. What's the connection to when and how you can cloak?"

"It's just easier for me if I'm an extension of the vehicle."

"But you were in the vehicle anyway," she noted, "so ..."

He shrugged. "I'm never a passenger. It just wasn't the same thing."

She nodded. "I wondered if it was something like that. Anyway, I don't know that Brody himself figured it out, but maybe you should do the driving from now on." Brody frowned at her, opening his mouth, but she went to pinch him again, and he held up both hands in mock surrender.

Legend gave her a half smile. "Yes, ma'am."

"Also," she added, looking over at Blair, "you can't protect Larry from everything."

"I know that." Blair gave her a lopsided grin. "You're also the one protecting him."

"I was keeping him asleep, trying to divert some of this

nightmare away from him, but we can't keep it all away from him. Right about now he probably knows more than any child of that age should. But the fact of the matter is, you are still protecting him, and he needs to develop some of that protective spirit himself."

"Fine, but do you really think he needs it reduced *now*, with all this going on?"

At that, Clary gave her a warm caring smile. "It's one of the reasons I was wondering about bringing the whole lot of you my way. I need to ask the others about it."

"The last thing you need is to have me and Larry there," Blair noted. "It's one thing if Larry and I have a home someplace, where he can get back to school and his studies and slowly heal. However, it's another thing entirely to throw us into the mix because they want Legend."

"I think it's very important that Legend is still in Larry's life," Clary stated.

"Sure," Blair agreed. "So maybe Larry needs to go with Legend and without me."

Legend immediately protested. "I'm not sure just what Clary's suggesting here, other than that you come for a visit."

"I would be your brother's caregiver," Blair stated, "and I don't think that they have the room, time, or energy for me to come in that capacity."

At that, Clary laughed. "Oh, there's definitely the energy," she quipped, "but it's probably scattered all to hell and gone by now," she muttered. "Anyway, let's all get some sleep, and we'll talk in the morning."

LEGEND, AFTER THE two gunmen had been picked up and

removed, sat outside in the darkness. Hearing a sound beside him, he shifted his senses and realized it was Brody. "One of us needs to get some sleep," Legend murmured.

"I was thinking you would stand watch," Brody said, "but I wanted to double-check."

"I'm not feeling quite comfortable enough to ignore the fact that there could be other attackers," Legend admitted.

"No, me neither," Brody agreed, "and I heard the women talking earlier about a similar possibility."

"Of course," Legend grumbled. "As much as we want to think that this is over, my father commanded many millions of dollars, and there will be a lot of people who think they deserve a piece of the pie, now that he's a prisoner."

"Not a prisoner anymore."

"Damn, I forgot," he muttered under his breath. "Now that he's deceased."

"I'm sorry, man. Despite how it went, he was your father."

"He was, but he wasn't someone I could ever agree with, and we could never come to any kind of a meeting of the minds. You have no idea how hard I tried to convince him to stop this foolishness, but he was adamant that victory was his."

"Was he just delusional?"

"I don't know." Legend gave a wave of his hand. "At some point in time, he had some psychic tell him that he would rule the world, and I think that may have gone to his head."

"*Yeah*," Brody agreed. "That is the kind of thing some psychic would say but not necessarily what anybody needs to hear."

"Particularly somebody who is already power hungry,"

Legend murmured. He glanced back inside. "Is everybody asleep?"

"They are. That brother of yours is sure something, and, according to the women, he's even more special because of how ill he'd been."

"I guess whatever methods were used to keep him alive ... maybe changed him somehow."

"Yes, I understand from Clary that he's picked up quite a bit of that same healing energy, and he's connected to her in many ways."

Legend didn't say anything. What could he say? It made sense, and it was a hazard of the kind of work the woman did.

"She also seems to think that you're extremely powerful as well."

Legend snorted at that. "Now that just gives me shudders and memories of my father's words."

"Right. Sorry, I didn't quite mean it that way."

"Good thing," he declared, his tone turning hard, "because I am definitely not like my father."

"Neither is your brother."

"Absolutely not, and it about killed me when Larry admitted to feeling guilty for being relieved to be free to just be himself. Relief from all that pressure to be someone he is not. I totally get it and honestly feel the same way."

"Nothing quite like parents to mess us up."

"I think a huge part of our whole experience in this lifetime has to do with learning from all the screwups that happened while we were children," Legend shared.

"I hadn't considered that." Brody stepped forward, sniffed the air, and muttered, "It seems calm."

"Yeah, but I don't trust it."

"I know. I'll go catch four, and I'll come back and relieve you then." Without waiting for an acknowledgment, Brody turned and headed back inside.

It was a matter of trust, as in realizing that, if Brody were needed, Legend would call him. So, since Brody wasn't needed at the moment, he would let Legend take first watch, and Brody would relieve Legend on the next one. It was a system that each of them had always used, but Legend had never worked with Brody before. Yet it had been natural for Legend to step out and to take first watch. Some things you just didn't let go of. Besides, Larry was his brother, and that was not something Legend would forget easily.

He got up and wandered toward the lake a few feet, his own senses highly upturned, as he listened for any intruders or for anything else that would disrupt the peace and quiet of the night. The conversation and questions from the cops had been kept to a minimum, once they realized who the kidnappers had been, and the gunmen were quickly bundled up and taken away.

Everything was on a hush-hush basis, so that the current government could minimize the political fallout from people finding out that there'd actually been a coup attempt. Legend had listened in on the news, and there was definitely some coverage, more so now that it had been apparently squashed, but Legend wished he could get the actual truth.

It wouldn't happen, and he knew that, but it still pissed him off to see that, no matter what government it was out there, there was still corruption, still coverups, or anything else you wanted to call it. He headed back toward the trees, taking a moment to examine the area around them, then surveyed the cabin and the surrounding areas.

There was a disquiet, just a whisper of unease rifling

through his system, yet he couldn't see any reason for it, couldn't see a direction. He wondered just what value his brother would be to somebody else and whether this would be an ongoing concern. Would there actually be an end in sight for all this? What the hell was Legend supposed to do as a guardian?

He was glad Blair had agreed to stay on at least for a time, but, already in the back of his mind, he knew how badly he needed her to maintain some consistency with his brother. That Legend didn't have a place or a job anymore was a whole different story. After he had skipped out without a word or a note for his former team to rescue his brother, Legend knew full well that he was no longer welcome back there. For all he knew, they may have thought he was captured or even helping his father with his coup. Legend sighed.

Consistency meant having a home, a place where Larry felt safe, where they wouldn't be looking at everybody else possibly attacking them. But to find that, and to set it up, wouldn't be easy. It would be a whole different story. With Legend being footloose and fancy-free, none of that had mattered to him, … until now. He kept a small apartment in London as a base, but it wasn't big enough for two of them, no matter three of them. Yet Legend could see that, with a ten-year-old, it would be a whole different ball game.

He continued to walk around the cabin area, looking to find what had disturbed him, but again, it was just a whisper, just that brush of a hand across the nape of his neck, making the hair stand up, telling him something was going on, something he didn't like one bit. Just on the off chance, he put his phone on Silent, so nobody would disturb him or give away his position. Then he shifted and came around to the front of the property.

Other cabins were here, other people, yet they seemed to be on holiday or the hard-partying crowd. So far, Legend and the others here hadn't had any communication with those outside of their group, other than the odd hand in the air from a distance. They seemed all right, but they weren't anybody Legend was interested in getting too friendly with, not given their current situation. Not that he was the overly friendly type anyway.

He'd always been more of a loner, but then, when you had a father hell-bent on taking over the world, regardless of the governments in play, it tended to put a damper on relationships in Legend's life. Not that he'd had a whole lot to do with his father either. That was the other part.

There wasn't anything to legally compel him to look after his brother, but Legend couldn't *not* do it. He was close to his brother, and this could be his one chance to actually connect and continue to build their relationship and to hopefully give Larry a chance for a much better life than Legend had had. It didn't seem that Legend was destined to have a family himself, so maybe forming a little family with Larry would be a good thing for both of them.

Frowning at the wayward thoughts rambling through his head, he took one more step forward, right when a branch crackled off to the side. He froze and waited, letting his gaze shift in the darkness. His senses were wide open, yet he couldn't see anything, and that was bothersome. Either somebody was using a methodology to hide their own tracks, in which case Legend had bigger problems than trying to find a place where his brother could stay, or his own senses were being dulled by something. Also not something he wanted to consider. His mind raced, searching for any clue.

Just as he was about to relax and put it down to wildlife or Mother Nature, he heard another crackle, this time a very defined footfall. He shifted his vision through the darkness to his right, where the sound had come from, then barely made out a shadow moving toward the cabin. He sent out an alert, hoping that somebody would be there to receive it. Otherwise he would grab his phone. But, with so many people out here talking energy, surely somebody would be aware. It was too early for Brody to come in for his shift change, though that was actually a good thing because he needed as much sleep as he could get too.

When a voice slammed into his brain, he shuddered in place, nearly giving away his position with the movement. It was Terkel.

I've alerted Brody, Terk stated, his tone calm.

Instinctively Legend slammed back with *Turn down the volume.*

With almost a note of laughter, Terk replied, *That's controlled on your side*, and with that, he disappeared.

Swearing under his breath, Legend quickly modulated the volume in his head, wondering at Terkel's ability to just step into somebody's mind and step back out again. They would have a serious talk when this was over, and they would also have some ground rules, if Legend decided to work for him.

You're already working for me, Terkel noted, his tone now much softer inside Legend's brain. *You just don't know it yet.*

Have to survive this first, he snapped.

One or two?

I only see one, but that means nothing.

No, it sure doesn't. You know that your brother will be one hell of a man.

If he lives that long.

I hear you there, Terk agreed in a contemplative mood. *I don't know if you know it, but Clary brought up bringing you guys here earlier today.*

I'm sure that went over well.

Nobody wants to see a child hurt, but we can't be an orphanage either.

Considering Legend was busy following the predator in front of him, he added, *Can we talk about his later? I'm on the move to the cabin.*

Got it, Terk replied. *As I mentioned, I already told Brody, so there is a welcome wagon waiting for your intruder.*

Yeah, well, he's got at least one gun, if not a second, and he's carrying a knife in his boot pocket, Legend pointed out. *I can just see the metal because it's sitting at the top.*

I'll pass that on, but you can talk to Brody this way too, and, with that, Terkel was gone.

The thought of telepathically talking to Brody wasn't exactly at the top of Legend's list, but, if it would keep him and Larry alive right now, Legend was game. Besides, it was a hell of a hidden weapon if they could make this work. He sent out an alert to Brody and gave him the details on the weapons.

Brody's voice came back calm and quiet. *Got it.*

And, with that, Legend had to be satisfied. He was putting an awful lot of trust in these people and their skills, but then they were putting a lot of trust in him too. Basically that's what teamwork was, It had been hard to walk away from his former team, friends he knew and trusted, but harder still to trust on a completely new level with people he didn't know, yet who had abilities that were shocking. If they could do even half of what Legend suspected, he'd be a fool to not take Terkel up on his offer.

Damn right, Terkel agreed. *Keep that in mind. Clary's on watch now too.*

Legend wasn't even sure what that meant, but, as he stepped closer toward the cabin, he saw the predator coming around to the side door, his handgun out, shifting so he could look in the window. The window itself was open, which Legend didn't remember from earlier, but, with the heat of the day, it made sense that somebody had opened it. As the guy peered around the corner, a fist caught him hard in the face, before Brody stepped out of the door to tackle him. Legend was on him within seconds. As they picked up the guy and carted him into the cabin, Legend quickly pocketed the guy's knife, while Brody took care of the handgun.

Legend looked at the guy, shook his head, and said, "I don't even know who you are."

"You weren't supposed to find out either," he muttered. "Now I'll be in deep shit."

"Yeah, well, anybody who comes to try and attack us won't do any better," Legend stated, his voice hard. "What the hell is going on?"

He shrugged. "Let's just say that everybody knows the kid's father is dead, and now people want a piece of the pie."

"What's that got to do with the kid? He doesn't have any ability to take care of that," Legend asked in bewilderment. "Why would anybody attack the kid?"

"Because he is set to inherit a fortune, and whoever controls the kid controls the fortune."

Well hell. Legend hadn't looked at it from that point of view.

At that, Brody swore, then he looked over at Legend. "We need to get that paperwork taken care of."

Legend nodded, his face grim. "Yeah, let me make some phone calls, and I'll get it started."

And, with that, he stepped outside, contacted both the lawyer and the house manager, plus made calls to the contact people at several banks. They hadn't expected to do this so quickly, but Legend was the guardian, and that meant it came down to him. The problem was, if something happened to Legend, who could step in and take over again? They'd have to set up some system to keep Larry safe, which had suddenly started to look like a full-time job—and a hell of a job at that.

CHAPTER 9

HEARING THE COMMOTION, Blair woke up, then snuck out to the living room to see a stranger collapsed on the floor, with both Brody and Legend standing over him, glaring. "Another attacker?" she murmured, as she joined them.

Legend nodded. "Yes, found him outside."

"So you did stay on watch, didn't you?"

"Of course." He shrugged. "Instincts."

"Yeah, your instincts are pretty good," she confirmed. "I was just so tired. I needed to sleep."

"Which is why we're taking shifts."

She looked down at her cell phone and shuddered at the time but resolutely headed for the teakettle.

"You might as well just go back to bed," Brody suggested.

She shook her head and sighed. "I'm awake now. Besides, something else is going on here. I don't know how much of all this you guys have figured out, but I can't say I'm terribly impressed."

"What do you mean?" Brody asked, looking confused.

"There's a reason why they're coming after Larry, which I get. Money is involved," she said, with a wave of her hand. "But he's still a child, and sure it's easy to assume that controlling the child means controlling the money, but that's not even true. Plus, how did they find us quickly? They've been after us since before we really even left the mansion. This doesn't seem like random opportunists to me. Surely someone is behind it."

At that, Brody looked at her with respect. "Yeah, I don't disagree with you on that. Do you have any idea who?" he asked. "After all, you're the one who was living there."

She winced. "Not a reminder I particularly care to have brought up," she muttered. "But, yes, I did live there, and definitely people were around. I guess the person to talk to would be the manager. He's … I mean, I called him the manager, but he was kind of what they called the man of affairs because he handled everything."

At that, Brody looked at her, with a suddenly sharp gaze. "What kind of man is he?"

She stared back at him, surprised. "I would have said fine, but I didn't really have any dealings with him. I got my paycheck on time, and, if we needed anything for Larry's care, like clothing or things for school, I'd ask him for the money to get it."

"Would he just hand it over or what?"

"Yes," she stated, with a nod. "Cash, usually, or we had a credit card we could use. The limit was kept fairly low, and, if we needed to go above that, then I just had to ask."

"Were you ever turned down?"

"No, never. The kid could pretty well have or do whatever he wanted."

"What did Larry like to spend money on?" Legend asked from the doorway.

She turned to face him. "Honestly, schoolbooks."

Legend smiled. "He really does like his studies, doesn't he?"

"He loves them. He loves school. That would be the one thing I especially worry about. If anybody took that away from him, I could see him slowly crumbling. Anything else, he's pretty resilient. He would cheerfully never get dressed or shower on a day-to-day basis, yet, if he had his way, he would always be at school. And I don't know if you know this, but he's intelligent," she added as an afterthought, "as in seriously intelligent. Genius level perhaps."

"Clary mentioned he has a special energy, and you reckon he's a bona fide genius." Brody nodded. "Great, so what are we looking at here? Larry comes up with a future cure for cancer or some such thing?"

She smiled. "I wouldn't laugh about it because it's quite possible."

He sighed. "Yeah, but only if we can keep him alive. It's a little hard to convince people of something like that."

"There's no need to convince anybody," she declared. "Guys like this, they only want money." She nodded to the prisoner, who was staring at them both with interest. "The thing is, how does he expect to get cash from the kid, unless somebody out there is offering money for the kid." She looked at Brody, with a raised eyebrow. He just shrugged and didn't say anything. She looked back at Legend. "You don't have much in the way of scruples. Do you want to beat him up for me?"

Legend stared at her, with a tilt of his head. "I don't?" he asked in a dry tone.

She shrugged. "I suspect, when push comes to shove, you would be happy enough to see this guy in another dimension."

"Well, I don't know about *another dimension*," he clarified, his eyebrow shooting up, "particularly if I'm using it to come back, but sure I could have some fun making him talk. Still, I can't say I like your way of putting it though," he muttered, as he walked forward.

At that, the newest gunman shifted uneasily in his chair.

She looked down at him. "And you know about all this gangster stuff, don't you?" she asked the gunman. "It's the stuff you always did for Mr. Kartal, right? I mean, you're probably just one of the many henchmen who took care of a certain corner of his life and always expected to get paid for it."

"I did," he replied, "until he lost this war."

"Did you really think he would win this one?"

He shrugged, then nodded. "Hell yeah."

"Interesting," she murmured. She looked over at the others. "Everybody seems to have been so steady in his corner. Yet I wonder if it was just a code or a belief or if Mr. Kartal really had that kind of ability, and something just went wrong."

"He was betrayed," the prisoner stated. "One of his own people, but we don't know who."

"That really sucks," she noted quietly, "at least for him."

"And also for you," he declared, looking up at her. "You're the nanny. You were disposable, just like us."

She winced at that. "*Thanks*, that's always nice to know."

He shrugged. "That's just the world that we live in."

"That's the world *you* live in," she snapped. "I was busy working with Larry, teaching him."

"Right, but you were supposed to be a nanny, not a tutor."

"I was both," she corrected him absentmindedly, "but that's neither here nor there."

At that, Legend walked forward and asked, "Who hired

you?"

"Nobody," he replied, "but there's …" He hesitated and then shrugged.

"What?"

"Well, if I won't get it, somebody else sure as hell will."

"Get what?"

"The bounty. On the kid. Bring him back alive for $250,000."

At that, Blair winced. "Well, at least now we know what he's worth."

"Oh, he's worth a lot more than that to the right person," the prisoner declared, with a shrug. "I won't get a chance at that kind of money, even though I came close." He glared at Legend. "How the hell did you even know I was out there?"

"It's what we do," he said, with a hard smile. "How many people know about this bounty?"

At that, he laughed. "Everybody within the group."

"How many?"

"Probably twenty, although I understand you've taken out a couple."

At that, Legend swore, and Brody even stared at him. "Are we seriously thinking we'll have to deal with something like seventeen more potential assassins?"

"I want to know who is behind it," Blair stated. "That seems to be the bigger issue here. If we can get him to pull the bounty, we can get out of this."

"You'd like to think so, wouldn't you?" The gunman snorted.

"Who posted it?" Brody asked, glaring at the prisoner.

He hesitated, then grunted. "We're not exactly sure. It was posted anonymously but within the ranks. We have a group of twenty of us, and we've all been working there for quite a while. We didn't think anything of it, until this announcement came out. Not knowing who put it out, we also didn't know how many people we would be racing against for the prize, but most of us came looking for it."

"Of course you did. That's a fair chunk of money, isn't it?"

"Yeah, you're not kidding. For those of us who are looking to get the hell away right now, it's escape money, with a chance to relocate somewhere else."

"If you've been associated with Mr. Kartal all this time," Blair noted, "obviously you have some decent money of your own set aside. There must be."

"Well, some people moved their money ahead of time just in case, but others didn't, and assets of those known accomplices have been frozen. Unfortunately I'm one of those."

"So," Blair added, "the government knows about you, and, therefore, maybe they'll pay us to get you back."

The gunman stiffened at that and glared at her.

She shrugged. "I mean, the kid's got to have his future paid for, and, while all you guys are busy trying to kidnap him, who the hell is helping him out?"

"He's got lots of money."

"Not necessarily," Brody pointed out. "It depends on who'll end up owning some of that property. If it was gained by stolen funds, you know the kid won't have a whole lot left in the end."

At that, the prisoner nodded. "That's quite possible. If the government ever figures it all out and gets a hold of what he took from everybody, they'll see that a lot of those funds belong to the people."

"*Great*," Blair muttered. "It won't be fun telling him that." When Brody looked at her with a cocked eyebrow, she explained, "He'll want to give it back to the people."

Brody chuckled, shaking his head. "I'm liking this kid more and more already."

"He's a good kid, and he'll certainly need enough to get through life, but he won't want to keep anything that could have come through his father's ill-gotten gains, particularly if the people were hurt by it."

At that, the prisoner looked at her in surprise and then smirked. "Do you really think any of his stuff came through hard work? He got it all through blackmail, through murder, through jobs of the worst kind," the gunman shared. "He's been so successful up until now, and not one of us thought anything of it. We all headed down this pathway, knowing that he would be the next president."

"Until somebody turned you in."

"Well, until somebody turned *him* in," the gunman clarified. "Still, I find myself wanting to find that bastard and take him out myself."

"For yourself or out of loyalty to your leader?" she asked curiously.

He shrugged. "Both. It could have been a good gig for me too."

She couldn't even imagine what life would be like if these guys had taken over the country. "Well, the bottom line right now," she said, looking over at Brody, "is that we need to find out who posted the bounty. We need to get that revoked, and the kid needs to be stashed somewhere safe, until he's old enough to make decisions on his own—if he even gets an option to make a decision."

"That's the problem," Legend noted. "Right now we're

doing paperwork. He can make a decision after the fact, once he's had a chance to go over everything. It's not all stolen money. Some of it came from Larry's mother. Unfortunately I suspect that he married her just to get her money, and frankly I've always wondered if he didn't have something to do with her death because, aside from the money, she was nothing but a pain in the ass to him."

"That's exactly how it happened," the prisoner confirmed, with a laugh. "He had no time for women, unless they had a purpose."

"He didn't have the time for *anybody*, unless they had a purpose," Legend corrected.

At that, their captive looked at him closely. "You're Legend, aren't you? His son, his disappointing son."

"Yeah, disappointing because I wouldn't stand by his side while he tried to steal the country from the people."

The gunman shrugged. "There have been coups since time began," he muttered, "so I don't know why you have to be so fussy about it right now."

"I'm not," he countered, with half a smile. "I just don't believe in playing games based on power and greed, especially when it involves other people's lives."

The prisoner laughed. "I could tell you who I think the traitor is, but I'll want something for it."

"Yeah, what do you want?" Blair asked, looking over at him.

He shrugged. "I need to get out of here for one, freedom for another, and money to survive of course."

She nodded absentmindedly. "Of course that's *all* you want"—she gave a fake laugh—"as if we have nothing better to do."

"You've got the kid's fortune to control," he noted.

"That's huge in itself."

"Is it though?" she asked, looking over at Legend. "Seems like an awful lot of people want to control it—and him." Legend just nodded. Blair faced the prisoner but went silent.

"Better decide fast. Not much time to think about it," the prisoner warned. He opened his mouth and started to laugh. "Besides …"

Splat.

LEGEND RACED OUT of the house, disappearing into the shadows. He knew instinctively that Brody would go out the other direction, leaving the two women with the body of their prisoner, who no doubt was dead. Whoever had fired the shot had blown off half his head. At the same time, if he were somehow still alive, not much of anything could be done for him. Clary would have to hold down the fort inside, while Legend and Brody worked the perimeter.

What Legend wanted was the damn shooter. If there were some fifteen *more* people still out here, it would be a nightmare that would have no end because half of those could go undercover for a time—years even—sinking into the shadows, only to pop up at any point in the future, when they thought the circumstances were better. Legend was not prepared to live with that, and it was definitely something his younger brother should not have to tolerate.

Moving as silently as possible, while still at full speed, Legend raced to the road on the other side, where the cabin property stopped. There he came to a halt and tuned up his hearing. He heard a vehicle revving up ever-so-slightly, as if somebody was impatiently waiting for someone to return. Noting that, Legend quickly turned in that direction and snuck around, until he came up behind the vehicle itself. Without any warning, he reached for the driver's door, opened it, and dragged the driver out onto the ground.

The guy cried out and curled up into a ball, his hands over his head. "I didn't do anything," he shrieked.

"Really?" Legend asked, his voice lethal. "I don't think I believe you."

"I didn't. I didn't. I was just supposed to wait for a guy to return. He just wanted a lift back into town."

"When was this?"

"Not very long ago, maybe half an hour?"

At that, Legend swore, realizing that this guy had been left as a decoy. "Would you recognize him? Did he leave you anything to identify him?"

"No, nothing. He had a hat on, and his collar was pulled up, as if he was really cold. He kept saying he'd be back in a few minutes, to just stay here and wait. Then I heard a gunshot, and I didn't know what to do."

"Well, I'll tell you what you'll do. You'll shut down this vehicle, and you'll come in and talk to the rest of us because he shot a prisoner we already had in our custody."

At that, the driver looked up at him, quivering. "A prisoner?"

Legend realized just how that sounded. "Yeah, a prisoner. As in the asshole shooter and his victim were both trying to attack a young boy in the cabin."

"What?" the driver asked in astonishment.

"First off, I want an ID on this guy."

"I don't have anything, nothing at all." At that, he started to cry. "Oh my God, am I in trouble for this?"

"I guess it depends on what you're doing here," Legend noted, stepping back and realizing that the guy really was just a decoy, and the asshole shooter was probably long gone. As Legend heard something and turned around, Brody slid out of the shadows. Legend called him over and explained what happened.

Brody looked at the driver in disgust. "What did he pay you?"

"One hundred bucks," he replied. "I'm trying to save money to go to college, so a hundred bucks is a lot."

"Yeah, I understand," Brody replied, "but now that hundred bucks just let a killer go free."

"But I didn't know," he cried out.

"Yeah, yeah," Brody said. He turned and looked around in the shadows. "I don't feel like he's here."

"No, but, if he isn't here, where the hell is he?" Legend asked. Then he looked over at the driver. "Is there any other way to get in or out of here?"

He nodded. "I mean, once you get to the highway, another one intersects it pretty quickly. He could easily have flagged down a ride, saying he was broken down or something," the driver muttered. "Honestly he asked me to stay though, so why would he do that?"

"Because it distracted us," Brody stated in disgust, "and we took the bait. Damn it."

Legend, just as grim, nodded. "Yeah, I hear you, and I agree. I don't feel like this guy's still around." He looked back at the driver. "But you're not going anywhere until we get a description."

"Six feet tall," he babbled. "Had a black jacket on, with the collar turned up, and he was younger maybe ..." Then he hesitated. "Well, I mean, way older than me, so like you guys' age."

"Did he say what he wanted?"

"He told me that he was checking to see if his girlfriend was meeting her lover here, and he just wanted to make sure. Honestly, when I heard the gunshot, I was afraid that he'd killed her."

"Well, he shot somebody. That's for sure. Did you see a weapon on him?"

The driver shook his head. "No, I wouldn't have picked him up if he'd had one in plain sight. I don't need that kind of headache."

"You don't need any of this," Legend declared, "but this is what happens when somebody wants to pay you one hundred bucks for a ride."

"Yeah, but it's not even that much by the time I pay for the gas."

"Where did you pick him up?"

"I was just coming out of classes. The college is about what? Maybe ten miles from here? He approached me and said that he needed a lift and that he was pretty upset."

"Did he look upset?"

The driver stopped and pondered that. "No, not really, he looked mad."

"Right, so chances are he was coming here, prepared for trouble," Brody replied.

"He brought a weapon," Legend noted, "and the only people doing that are the ones who are planning on trouble."

At that, Brody nodded. "Well, this guy still needs to talk to the authorities because we need this to end."

"Yeah, I hear you," Legend agreed, "but, in the meantime, we need to find out who the hell's behind all this shit."

"He did talk on the phone," the college guy offered suddenly.

At that, both men zeroed in on him. "What did he say?"

"He talked about a kid and how it better be for real. Otherwise somebody would pay."

"Did he give you a name?"

"He did, yeah. Hang on. Let me think." He considered it for a minute. "I think it was Richard."

Brody frowned. "Richard who? Did he give a last name or anything?"

The driver shook his head. "No, it was all about the kid."

"*Right*, well," Legend added, "I need to know everything you remember that he said. For that matter, we might as well take him back to the cabin and let the women talk to him."

Brody frowned, then nodded slowly. "I guess if anybody can get more information, it's them." He looked down at the driver and said, "Get into the passenger side." Brody quickly hopped into the driver's seat, with Legend taking the back seat, so he could keep an eye on the college guy, as they drove him to the cabin.

As soon as they got there, Clary stepped outside, her lips trembling.

Brody immediately wrapped her up in his arms. "I'm so sorry, sweetie."

She nodded, her gaze latching on to the newcomer. "Who's he?"

"He is the one who delivered our shooter," Brody replied. "He was paid a hundred bucks to bring him in."

Her shoulders sagged. "So, we're no closer, right?"

"No, we're no closer, but I wondered if you could get any more information from him."

She looked up at him, then back at the young guy,

shrugging. "Maybe. No guarantees though." She smiled at him and said, "Come on inside." Just as the guy went to walk in, she stopped him, looked over at Brody, and reminded him, "The body's still in there."

"We'll leave it there because the cops are on the way. We can't move him."

She nodded.

"We'll sit out here then," the driver called out nervously, avoiding even looking into the window. "I don't want to see it at all. I swear, I just … He asked me to bring him here, and I needed the money for school."

At that, she nodded. "I get it. When you were talking to him, do you remember any facial features, any scarring, tattoos, anything like that?"

"No. I mean, I was coming out of class, trying to get to my vehicle to go home. I was tired, worn out, and this guy … I didn't even want to get involved, but he sounded sincere. He seemed to think that his girlfriend was sleeping around, and he wasn't so much upset as he seemed angry."

"Right, and you said he talked on the phone once, and that was it?"

The driver nodded. "When he left, he looked back at me and told me to be very quiet. I'm not sure what he thought I would do that was noisy. All I had to do was sit there and wait for him."

"No, but you might have put on the music or something"—she frowned at him—"and that might have disturbed him."

"Right, well, I didn't do anything, so I'm really hoping I'm not in trouble," he muttered. "I really didn't intend for anything to happen, and I'm really sorry if somebody died."

"Well, somebody did die, and that's just where we're at

right now." Clary looked back at the others and shrugged. "I don't really think he knows anything more."

"He did mention the name Richard," Legend noted, "from a phone call."

"That's right," the driver said eagerly. "The guy said something about Richard would pay, if this wasn't for real."

"I wonder whether the shooter was here to collect the kid or to make sure that somebody else did the job, then disappeared when he realized the attacker had been caught. Either way, it's not great," Clary shared.

LEGEND HEARD A noise, and just then Blair stepped outside. Legend looked her over, while her gaze immediately went to him.

Seeing that he was okay, her shoulders relaxed.

He sighed because he felt the same damn way. It was confusing and frustrating, given the circumstances, but he walked over, put an arm around her, and asked, "Are you okay?"

She nodded, smiling up at him. "Now that I know you're fine, yeah," she said. "I sure wish this was over though." She turned and looked at the newcomer. "Who's he?" The explanation was fast and slightly truncated, but she got the message. "Right, so this guy gave the shooter a ride here, whether he was attempting to take Larry himself or was planning on shooting our prisoner anyway. But, if he was planning on taking Larry, no way he would have gone back to this guy with the child in tow. So, how the hell was he planning on getting out of here?"

At that, Legend eyed her. "That's a good point."

"Unless"—she winced, looking at the driver—"unless the shooter planned on shooting the driver, then taking his vehicle."

"That would make the most sense," Brody confirmed, with a nod.

"What?" As if he had just caught up, the college guy paled, his gaze widening in shock.

"Seems to me you've actually had a quick escape with your life," Blair noted, her voice quiet. "These guys will kill you. They seem nothing if not fully committed, all business and serious."

"What's even going on here?" the college guy asked.

She smiled. "We have a young boy I've been looking after for the last few years. His father's gotten into a hell of a lot of trouble, pissed off a lot of people, and now they're all expecting to grab the kid and use him for leverage to get money."

"Yeah, the guy mentioned leverage. Something about everybody'll use him for leverage. That's what the plan was for the child. Is that you guys too?" Then he glared at her suspiciously. 'That's not cool if you are."

She smiled. "You're right. It's not cool, and it's not what we were doing. We're protecting him. I've been looking after him for quite a few years now, and I sure as hell won't let some gunman come in here and take him because he wants money." She looked at him and asked, "Did he actually pay you?"

He nodded and pulled out a wad of bills.

"I suppose he had gloves on," Clary chipped in.

"Yeah, he did." Then he stopped and gasped. "I didn't even notice. God, I should have noticed, shouldn't I?"

"Well, it wouldn't have changed anything if you had,"

Blair replied. "I mean, think about it. If you'd noticed and made too much out of it, you might have got yourself shot earlier."

He winced at that. "*Great*, so being thick-headed and stupid actually saved my life."

"In this case it probably did," she agreed, with a nod. She looked up at the others. "Now what?"

"We have cops coming for the body and now to collect this guy," Legend murmured, "and we'll have to move again."

Blair pondered that and offered, "Or we just set up this place as a trap."

At that, Legend looked at her curiously. "I kind of like that idea, but we'd be putting other people in danger."

She thought about that. "We can always talk to whoever else might still be in the surrounding cabins here to see if they all want to disappear for a few days."

"And what is there to prevent this from being more than a few days?"

She wondered about that. "That's true. In that case, we need to go." She turned to the hopeless driver, who even now shifted uneasily, from one foot to the other. "So, this Richard? Did he sound like he was a friend or …"

He nodded. "At least like they knew each other pretty well. It was something about Richard would pay if something didn't happen."

"Right."

"Who is Richard?" Legend asked Blair in a low voice.

"I'm wondering if we don't have the property manager taking control of everything," she murmured. "If you think about it, he's the one who would be left to handle things, and, if he's put out a bounty on the kid, it's because he's got plans too."

"Yet you were laid off."

"I was, but how much of that came from your father?" she asked, looking up at him curiously.

"As to that, I have no idea, but you weren't terribly surprised."

"No, your father has always treated people like that. We're just numbers, people to do a job, and, when the job is done, get out of his life because he doesn't have time for you," she explained cheerfully.

Legend shook his head. "What an ass."

"Yeah, but not any longer."

"No, not any longer," he muttered. "Still, it doesn't feel right though. Unless this Richard guy is behind it all."

"Well, that would make sense, but then several other people must be in on it too."

He turned to her and asked, "Like who?"

"Well, think about it. Your father had a lot of business associates. He had a lawyer and an accountant. I mean, honestly those two could very easily be the ones with the power over all this. They're the ones who can move money quickly, legally, and lock it up," she pointed out. "If one of them was a questionable character, you can bet that they'll forget Larry and be focused on their own position."

Legend swore at that.

Blair continued. "Forget about that lawyer of his. I think he already has a record, at least I heard him whispering about he already had one strike against him, and a second wouldn't go down so well."

"No, it wouldn't. Why is it we always want the lawyer to be the guilty one?"

She burst out laughing at that. "Maybe, but what about

the accountant?"

"They could also be in cahoots," Brody suggested. "All kinds of opportunities exist here for people to get rich very quickly on money that's not their own."

"Really?" The college student looked from one to the other. "How is it that anybody can get rich on something like that?" he asked nervously. "I really don't want to hear what you guys are talking about."

"Oh, that's a good thing," Blair noted, as she stepped forward and gently touched his arm. "We're just trying to keep a young boy alive."

"But are you?" he muttered. "Because, you know, the way you're talking …"

"His father tried to overthrow the government, and he failed. He's been killed, and now everybody's trying to take over the boy's family money, and they're trying to do it by capturing him."

"Of course they are." The college student stared at her in shock. "What kind of world do you people live in?"

"Not that kind," she stated. "Honestly, we're just trying to keep his son alive."

He settled back somewhat and asked, "Do I really have to talk to the police?"

"I'm not sure there's any other choice," Blair replied. "If you think about it, you're the only one who saw the shooter."

He winced at that.

"Do you think any of the campus cameras would have picked him up?" Clary asked her husband.

"Tell me what college, and where you were exactly," Brody said to him. "We'll check it out."

And, with that, they quickly got the information from

him, and Brody headed inside with Clary. Legend and Blair stayed outside, waiting for the cops to arrive.

"The local cops will be kind of pissed at us, won't they?" she muttered.

Legend nodded. "Probably, but Terk already let them know what was going on, so the more we clear up for them, the less they have to do. They don't want to deal with any of it, since it ties into the bigger investigation on the coup. Not their jurisdiction, not their war."

"Maybe, but—"

"You don't want to set a precedent with something like this," Legend muttered.

"Hey, I don't want any of it," she whispered, standing close to his side. "I just wish this was well and truly over with."

"It will be, and soon, but we'll have to track down this Richard and confirm that whatever has been put up as a bounty is removed, or they can even say it's been claimed. Something that will send the mercenaries back where they came from."

"My passenger mentioned something like that too," the college student stated. "Something about mercenaries, but I didn't remember that until you said the word just now."

"What did he say?"

The college guy pondered it for a long moment, then shrugged. "Honestly I don't really remember, but it was something about every damn mercenary in the world being after the kid."

"True enough, our shooter was probably pissed off that he wasn't given a private job or an option to do it exclusively," Blair suggested.

At that, Legend nodded. "That's a good guess. The original poster may not have known who to call, so he just put it out among the team, instead of doing it privately, which would have been much more subtle."

"Guaranteeing we're in a lot more danger."

"Yes," Legend agreed. Just then, they heard the sound of a vehicle approaching, Blair stepped back into the shadows. The college student, seeing her reaction, tried to join her, but Legend grabbed him. "We'll just ensure that it's who we're expecting and not your guy coming back again."

"Jesus, if he is, I sure don't want to see him," the guy wailed.

"It won't matter if you want to or not. I hate to say it, but, if he thinks you're here, you'll be dead yourself."

At that, the college student froze, then tried to hide behind Legend. Luckily the police showed up, not the shooter.

When Blair stepped back out, Legend looked over at her questioningly, and she nodded. "I only get straight honesty here, so that's a good cop, with the coroner coming separately behind him."

"Terkel's team," Legend muttered. "They seem to have this wealth of personnel, with contacts around the world."

"Not sure it's so much *his* team as a collection of teams that work together," she muttered. "Still a good call for us."

By the time the explanations were done—with the college guy put in the cruiser, and the dead body removed—the early morning dawn was breaking through.

"So much for grabbing some shut-eye," Legend muttered.

"Your turn," Blair said. "I'm quite happy to stay up and keep watch."

He shook his head. "Yeah, that's not happening," he murmured. "You need sleep too, and, besides, what will you do if something does happen?" he asked in a scoffing tone.

She gave him a flat stare. "Nobody will hurt Larry while I'm around," she vowed.

CHAPTER 10

B LAIR WAS COMPLETELY sincere, but she could see from the look on Legend's face that he hadn't a clue how she meant it. "Look. Clary and I are both up, and we'll put on some coffee. For us. Not you. You need to go to sleep, at least grab yourself a couple hours."

He hesitated, feeling torn, but when she smacked him across the face, he gave his head a shake and asked, "What the hell? Did you do that?"

She nodded. "I sure did, and I'll do it again too," she muttered. "Your reflexes have gone to shit, so how are you going to protect Larry? Go get some rest while you can."

He glared at her. "How did you do that?"

"The same way you're out there cloaking things," she muttered. "You think you're the only one with abilities around here?"

He let out his breath slowly. "Seriously, you too?"

She nodded. "Yeah, me too, but then you knew that."

"No, but I'd wondered about it," he corrected. "Yet *knowing*, particularly on that level, is something very different."

She shrugged. "It's one of the reasons I work with Larry," she stated. "Clary started it because of all the healing, which left Larry very amenable to energy work, so it's part of what we do."

"So he's already learned a lot of this stuff?" Legend asked in astonishment.

"He hasn't had a choice. People are using him as a pawn, and, in a world of adults, nobody's giving a crap about the child involved."

He winced at that. "I know. Did my father know?"

"No. If he had, he would have exploited the poor kid all the more," she shared succinctly.

"I hate to say it, but you're right."

"I don't know what Larry's potential is, but he's an energy worker for sure. He cares more about healing people, probably because of what happened to him, but he's also manifested a lot of cloaking, and emotional energy. It's as he's trying out his use of energy as to what he can do, based on what he sees around him."

"I can see that, and you're right. We definitely need more healers in the world, and he will be amazing at anything he chooses to do. Keeping him safe won't be easy."

"No, we'll have to go back to whoever this Richard is and see what he's up to."

"I've got news on that," Brody announced, from behind them. She turned to see him standing there, with his hands on his hips, looking at the two of them.

"I thought you would have crashed by now," Blair said.

"Nah. Are you guys okay?"

"Sure," she replied, "as much as anybody caught up in this mess is okay, anyway."

"Good point," he muttered. "Come on in. We've got to talk." With that, Blair stepped inside, happy to find that Clary had put on coffee. "I suggested that Legend go get some sleep, but he's resisting."

"Of course he is," Clary said, with a shrug. "Yet hopefully he knows what he needs."

"He can go get a break after we discuss this update," Brody stated, "I got a few hours in last night, and Legend hasn't had a break yet."

Legend started to protest, but, when everybody shot him a quelling look, he conceded. "Fine, what did you find?" he muttered to Brody.

"This Richard appears to be part of your father's management team, not the one any of you have been dealing with all this time, but the one involved with Kartal's more underhanded dealings. He's also a lawyer, but not the one we were thinking of. He's been part of your father's team for over a decade, working in the shadows and keeping his dealings all the more mysterious. I think Kartal calls him Rip, doesn't he?"

At that, Blair nodded. "Now I know who you're talking about. He's somebody who doesn't like to be seen. He would come in and leave late at night, but I've seen him a couple times. He came up to take a look at Larry when he was first recovering, wondering how and why he had actually survived. I think he was fishing for information, particularly about Clary's role in all this, but I just told him that God worked in mysterious ways. He didn't seem to like that answer much and disappeared soon afterward, but he was not happy at all. I do remember that."

"That sounds like him. Maybe he was looking for somebody easy to manipulate."

"I'm not sure we did that good of a job of keeping a low profile when Larry survived," Clary added. "We were so damn happy that he was still with us, and so we assumed that everyone would be equally happy."

"Oh, I'm sure for the most part they were," Blair pointed out, "but I don't know that everybody had Larry's well-being at heart."

"No, of course not, and now it'll be even harder."

At that, Brody continued. "Terkel is searching for any information he can find on this guy. We have multiple addresses that he owns but, so far, not any he resides at."

"He was slimy," Blair stated. "He really kept to the shadows and didn't trust anybody."

"Well, that sounds very much like what we've got here now. We need to figure out whether he'll lay off or continue to hunt for Larry. Still, it would take the accountant and the lawyers to actually transfer most of this stuff anyway."

At that, Legend's phone rang. He got up and stepped away to answer it. Blair watched as he talked back and forth on the call. When he returned a few minutes later, he filled them in. "Documents are coming my way for transferring the properties out of Larry's name—or at least to add mine as guardian to them. So, once that is done, anybody trying to kill Larry still wouldn't get their hands on the assets, so hopefully that will help."

"Now all we need to do after that," Blair noted, looking at him, "is let the world know somehow. And you'll have to set up another beneficiary, in the case of your death, so that it's one more step away from Larry."

"Right." Legend nodded. "In that case I should set up a charity or something, so, no matter how many people they kill, the assets are still out of reach."

"Good point," Brody agreed. "You get that started, which will give us another degree of separation from anybody who's after Larry, and then we need to send a message to this Richard, though I'm not sure how to get that number."

They pondered the problem. "There should be some information at the house. At least within the known associates, somebody should know how to reach Rip, especially if Mr. Kartal is unavailable." Blair frowned. Then she pointed to the area where the dead guy had been. "Did you guys search the prisoner we had here?"

"We did," Legend said, "which reminds me." Hopping up, he pulled his phone from his pocket. "I took pictures of the guy's Contacts, and, sure enough, there's one called Bull's-Eye."

"Yeah, I take that as a good guess for our go-to guy," Brody replied.

Legend looked around at everybody. "We're in agreement to alert him then?" All nodded. "So, we set up this additional paperwork, transfer all the assets, then we let Rip know there is no hope of him getting at the money."

"But that'll still take a couple days," Brody noted. "Until the paperwork is done, we need to keep an extra eye out, until this is really something we can put out there."

Blair interrupted, "I don't want to put a damper on what is a good plan, but we also have to ensure he won't just kill Larry for the fun of it because he's pissed off." At that, everybody turned to look at her. She shrugged. "I don't think Rip's a very good loser."

"*Great*," Legend muttered, glancing at Brody. "So we go on the offensive and hunt him down?"

Brody nodded.

"Yes," Blair agreed, her voice serious. "That would be best. It's not an ideal answer, no matter which way we look at it. I'm coming with you though."

Legend shook his head. "No, you're not."

"Yes, I am, and don't go telling me what I can and cannot do. Besides, can you even identify Rip? Well, … can you?" she asked curiously.

Legend glared at her, and Brody laughed. "She's got a point."

"What will we do with Larry in the meantime?" Clary asked.

"We have Brody and Clary stay here with him, with extra protection," Legend muttered.

"Or we can take Larry back with us to headquarters," Clary suggested cheerfully. "I think he'll fit right in."

"What's that about?" Legend asked. "More pressure for me to join up so that my kid brother can stay?"

"Larry might get a spot even without you," Clary teased, sending a cheeky grin in his direction.

Legend groaned. "Look. First off, we have paperwork to deal with, and then we have to send the message. After that, we'll decide about where Larry should be, based on what kind of response we get from Rip."

"Sounds good," Brody said.

With a sigh, Legend stretched, then headed for the bedroom.

"Have a good sleep," Blair called out.

"Yeah, right," he muttered, then slammed the door shut, … a bit harder than necessary.

Blair chuckled. "He doesn't take suggestions well, does he?"

"None of us do," Brody admitted, "particularly when it comes to this kind of stuff."

"Yeah, well, it's not just you anymore," Blair muttered, as she stared at him. "Some of us can do things too."

At that, he stiffened, then turned and looked at her. "Are you an energy worker?" he demanded.

Blair looked over at Clary.

Clary shrugged, then added, "I haven't said anything."

"Yeah," Blair declared, looking at Brody defiantly. "Why?"

"I just want to know what I'm dealing with," he said, "because you're poking a tiger when you talk to Legend like that, and it can go wrong sometimes."

"Sometimes it can go wrong, but sometimes it can also go right. It all depends on which way he's leaning at any given time. I'd say that, right now, it's probably good to poke him."

"What is it you're trying to do when you poke at him?" Brody asked.

"Wake him up a bit and make him see me." She shrugged. "I've seen him off and on for years, but he never looks at me."

At that, Brody studied her, and he started to smile. "So, I was right," he exclaimed, then turned to his wife.

Clary smiled at him. "They still have quite a long way to go, dear."

"Maybe, but I was right."

"If it's important to you to be right," Clary noted, with that serene smile of hers, "then fine." He glared at her, and she chuckled.

"Glad to see that you guys sorted it out," Blair muttered, looking at them curiously. "It must be a challenge with the energy work."

"You would think it would be a challenge," Clary shared, "but seriously it should make things easier. While it wasn't easy to begin with, once we got there, it got better immediately."

Then suddenly a weird hum filled the air, and Blair

turned back to see the two of them looking at each other. "You can talk that way too, can't you?" she asked, clearly fascinated.

"Yes, so can Terkel," Brody said, with a wry look. "So, be warned. Just when you least expect it, you'll have Terk and anyone else on the team in your head too."

At that, Blair stared at him. "That's something I've never had experience with."

"None of us had because the bottom line is that Terkel is something special all on his own," Brody admitted. "We have yet to see anybody who can equal him."

"It's not about equaling him," Blair clarified. "It's about finding the best way to complement each other."

Brody chuckled. "Yeah, you'll fit right in," he said, yet with a headshake. "I don't know if the rest of the place is ready for it though." Brody looked back at Clary.

"Probably not," Clary agreed quietly, "but it is one of the things that we wanted to do."

"You've lost me," Blair said, looking back at her. "What does that mean?"

"We were looking for more team members, which is why we're trying to convince Legend to join us," she explained. "There's always a need for good men."

"Yeah, I can see that," Blair muttered, "but he's difficult, and you know that already."

"We have more than a few difficult people in our group," Brody noted, with a laugh. "Plus there's Riff, another potential team member, who kind of comes in and out of our world, not necessarily on our time frame."

"Not sure any of them would come in on your time frame," Blair admitted, with a smile. "Sounds to me as if they're all just as stubborn and as cantankerous as you are."

He stared at her in shock and asked, "How do you know I'm any of those things?" he protested.

She shrugged. "You're male, and this is the kind of work you do. I think it goes along as a package deal." She looked over at Clary. "Am I right or what?"

"Oh, you're right," she stated, chuckling at the look on Brody's face. "But, as I said, we've come a long way together."

"I'm glad for you," Blair replied sincerely.

Clary nodded. "I don't think there's anything better than realizing you have a second half of yourself who's equally adept at energy. That's so very important when it's the same work you do."

"There's more than a few of us out there," Blair muttered, glaring at the door where Legend had disappeared.

"You'll get there," Clary added. "Just give it time."

She looked over at her, smiled a sad smile, and shared, "Well, he's been in and around in the background for years now and has never shown any interest. ... So, as far as I'm concerned, he's had all the time he'll get. It's either a sledgehammer over the head or a whack."

At that, Brody grinned broadly. "Given that it's Legend, I would say the sledgehammer would be more like it."

LEGEND HAD SLEPT long and hard. One of his abilities was to recharge relatively quickly, though he didn't even really know what other abilities he had because he'd never been in a position of having to identify them. Like who did that? Did you sit down and say, *Go invisible. Check.* No. He just went through life one day at a time, dealing with all these corrupt nations and people, working for a couple of good bosses and a couple who were not so good.

Terkel would be a good boss. Legend was just undecided about it because of his energy thing. It was very invasive, and the one thing Legend did like was his privacy. But, as he stumbled out of the bedroom to join the others, everybody sat around their laptops, sipping coffee.

Blair gave him a glare.

He glared right back. "I slept."

"You were only down for an hour."

"But, for me, that's as good as four."

She faced him, assessed something about him, and then nodded. "There's still coffee."

"Glad to hear that. Otherwise I would put on fresh. Did you guys come to any decision?" he asked, pouring a cup of coffee and now coming toward them.

"All kinds of decisions," Brody declared, with a level of cheerfulness that made Legend suspicious. "Not sure any of them involved your cooperation though."

"Well, all of them will involve your cooperation to put them into play," Blair clarified, with a cheeky grin, "but we won't discuss them with you."

He frowned at her and at Brody, then turned to Clary. "Clary, you want to make any sense of this?"

She chuckled. "It's all good."

Just then from behind Legend, Larry came out of his bedroom, rubbing his eyes.

Blair got up and walked over to him. "Hey, sleepyhead. How are you doing?"

He looked up at her, blinking. "I'm hungry."

"Yeah, that's about normal," she muttered. "What will you have?"

"Food, lots of it."

"Yeah, but your version of food and *lots* may not be the same as mine," she noted, "so can you be a little more specific?"

"I would like three scrambled eggs, bacon, ham, and toast, I guess."

"Well, you can have the scrambled eggs, bacon, and toast, but we don't have any ham."

He stopped, as if suddenly realizing where he was. "Oh, right." Then he turned, caught sight of his brother, and grinned. "Hey, you're still here," he said enthusiastically.

"Yeah, I'm still here. Did you expect me to run and hide or something?"

"No, not run and hide, but you generally don't stick around very long."

A note of … not quite sadness but something in Larry's tone made Legend realize that maybe his little brother had missed him more than Legend had realized. "Sorry, big guy. Sometimes life gets a little crazy."

"Yeah, it sure does." Larry nodded. "Do we have any updates?"

"Lots," Blair replied, "and you slept through all the action."

"Yeah, there was definitely an odd feeling to the room," he noted, with a shiver. "Maybe that's why I'm extra hungry."

"Do shivers make your appetite build?" Legend asked curiously. Larry looked over at him, then turned to Clary.

She nodded and said, "It's fine to tell him."

"Is it though?"

"Yes," she declared, with a clarity that seemed to reassure him.

Larry turned to Legend. "So, whenever there's bad energy around, I burn through a lot of my own energy. I just don't know why yet."

Legend studied him carefully and suggested, "Maybe you're looking for the enemy. Maybe you're trying to protect the place, without even thinking about it. You care so much that you're stretching yourself, and it's burning through your energy faster."

Larry considered him and his words, then said, "It could be either of those, but I fall asleep every time I'm trying to sort it out. Clary and Blair keep telling me to ease up on it, and I will figure it out, but it's really erratic still."

At that, Blair headed into the kitchen to make breakfast.

"It's probably a part of your age as much as anything," Legend suggested.

Larry shot him a disgusted look. "Yeah, I've heard that a few times too. They seem to think it's got something to do with hormones."

Such disgust filled Larry's tone that Legend burst out laughing. "Yeah, sorry about that, bud, but it's all part and parcel of growing up."

"Well, it sucks," Larry stated. "I personally think we should grow up when and how we want to, without any of that nonsense part of it."

"Well, if that works out for you, let me know because, so far, I can't say I've seen it happen too many times."

"Yeah, it won't happen," Larry muttered, as he walked over and plunked himself down on a chair next to his brother, "but, in the meantime, I'll eat anything that's coming my way."

"Well, that'll be nice for a change," Blair noted from the kitchen. "Usually you're on the picky side."

"Too hungry to be picky now," he mumbled. Then he yawned and looked around, bleary-eyed. "Why am I still tired?"

Clary smiled. "Hey, sometimes you just need some re-charging time."

"*Maybe.*" Then Larry looked at her suspiciously. "Did you knock me out again?"

"Nope, I sure didn't," she replied. "Do you want me to?"

Such an overstated mock threat filled her voice that he looked at her and giggled. "You know that is actually pretty cool that you can do that."

"Yeah, it is pretty cool." Then in a mock whisper, she added, "It also helps keep Brody in line."

"Hey, hey, hey," Brody protested. Then, hopping to his feet, he barged into the kitchen, sniffing around. "Are you making enough for everyone or just for the hungry kid? I could use some breakfast too."

And, with that, a raucous breakfast began.

CHAPTER 11

S EVERAL HOURS LATER, after everybody had eaten, after the kitchen had been cleaned up, they were mostly packed. "I still don't know what the plan is," Larry said almost petulantly, speaking from the kitchen counter, where he'd parked his butt. "Why can't we just stay here until it's all settled?"

"Well, so far, four armed people have found us, plus the clueless driver, so that's hardly a good solution, and we can't afford to have this Richard guy come back with somebody else."

"But he will," Larry stated, "as long as he thinks there's money in it."

"Which is why I'll go off and pay him a visit," Legend shared.

"Yeah, you and what army?" Larry muttered. "You know Dad's got a whole army, right?"

"Yeah, I do know that," Legend confirmed. "He wanted me to join it at one time."

"But you didn't want to?" Larry asked, cautiously looking at his older brother.

"No, I sure didn't. That's not my style."

Larry studied his face. Then came a weird buzz of energy, as if he were searching to see if his brother was lying. Then he relaxed. "Well, that's good." Larry looked over at

Clary. "I don't think I should go back to your place. That'll just bring trouble your way."

"Yeah, it might," she admitted, "but I've talked to the others, and they're totally okay with it."

"Are they really okay with it, or are they just hoping it will force my brother into working for you?" Larry asked, with an adult perception that made Blair stop and look at him closely.

"Even if they are," Clary explained, "your brother is perfectly capable of telling them *Thanks, but no thanks* and taking you off to another place."

"Why should I have to go with him anyway?" Larry questioned, his belligerence mounting.

"Because your father appointed Legend as your guardian," Blair added, knowing that she had just dropped a bomb.

Larry stared at her in horror, then turned to look at Legend, who was off on the other side of the room, listening but staying out of the conversation as much as he could. At that, Larry lowered his voice to a hushed whisper, "Why would he do that?"

"I believe your dad did it because he knew that Legend would keep you safe," Blair replied, her voice just as inflexible as Legend's had been earlier.

Larry stared at her, and then his shoulders slumped, but he nodded too. "That much is true."

"I'm glad you accept that much," Legend stated, walking over. "Listen. I didn't have much warning about this either, so I can't say I have any answers for you, but together we'll limp along and get through it somehow."

"*Somehow* is right," Larry muttered. "Because look at you now. ... You're about to take off, so where does that leave me?"

"It leaves you with me," Blair declared. "The same as it always has."

At that, he looked at her hopefully. "You didn't get fired?"

"Well, let's just say that, for the moment, I'm still on the job," she replied.

Larry shook his head. "You can't work for nothing," he muttered. "The world doesn't work that way. You taught me that."

"I'm not working for nothing," she stated. "I'm getting paid. The details of how and what isn't really a discussion you need to be a part of."

He glared at her. "Oh, we're back to that 'need to know' crap, *huh*?"

"Ignoring the cussing issue, here's my reply. No, not at all, since I consider my finances personal and private."

At that, Larry looked ashamed. "If there's one thing my father taught me, it was never to talk about money, so I'm sorry. I guess that was crossing the line."

She laughed. "You didn't cross the line because I didn't let you," she pointed out. "Remember? We all have boundaries, and my money, my income, and all the rest of that personal stuff of mine, is not up for discussion."

Larry nodded. "I guess I can understand that. I wish I knew if I had any money," he muttered.

"Well, you will have," Legend replied, "but that's part of what I still have to get sorted out."

"You mean money from Dad?" Larry asked.

"Partly. You also had money from your mother."

He frowned at that and then nodded. "I remember something about that, but Dad told me not to worry about it."

"Of course he did."

"There's a good chance he may have spent it," Larry noted, looking out the window.

"Listen," Legend began. "I'm hoping there's money, but, if there isn't, we'll figure it out. Regardless we'll get you a great education, and you can go from there."

There was a palpable easing of the tension in the room as Larry accepted Legend's words at face value. Blair was amused and yet relieved to see that a word from Legend could actually calm down his brother to this extent.

As he walked past her, dropping his bag of tools and whatnot at the front door, she told him in a low voice, "You could turn out to be quite useful."

He snorted. "Nice try. I've got to tell you that babysitting has never been my thing."

"Maybe not," she said cheerfully. "However, from now on, it had better become your thing."

And just enough of a note of a warning filled her tone to make him stop and look at her. "So you're not up for the job full-time?"

"Babysitting? No, not full-time. We'll talk about it later—once we get this nightmare over with," she murmured. "I have a life too, you know? At least I should have."

He pondered that for a moment and then acquiesced. "Fine, we'll talk about it afterward."

"As for now, of course, I'm coming with you." He froze, then turned and glared at her. She shrugged. "We're back to the same problem again. You don't know what Rip looks like. I do. I also know several of the other people involved in his shadier side of the business."

At that, Larry turned to him eagerly. "I could come. I know all the players too."

She smiled. "Well, that would kind of defeat the purpose. We don't want to actually deliver you back there, do we?"

His face fell. "I don't want you to go," he wailed.

"I know that," she noted, "but I also want you to be safe, not just for the moment but for the rest of your life." She got up, walked over to Larry, and asked him, "Have I ever let you down?"

He shook his head. "No."

"Have I ever lied to you?"

He shook his head again.

"So, believe me when I tell you that I will come back, and, when I do, we'll get busy and carry on with the physics."

His face lit up, as if she had offered him a major Christmas gift. "Really? You wouldn't lie to me, right?"

"No, I wouldn't lie to you. Physics it is, but we'll go solve this situation first. Then we'll come back, figure out where we'll be next and get settled, and then we'll resume the schooling. In the meantime, you still haven't finished the other homework I left you." She added just a note of severity to her tone to get him to realize that she meant it.

He groaned. "Well, if I would stop getting moved around, I could actually have a chance to open my books and to get something accomplished." He glared at her.

She smiled. "Very true, so this is your chance. We won't be gone very long, and, by the time we come back, we'll have some solutions."

He looked at her and then walked up, opened his arms, and gave her a hug. Not for the first time did she realize this ten-year-old was growing up at an almost alarming rate. Hugging him close, she whispered, "We'll be fine. I promise."

He nodded. "You know what will happen if you're not." There was a mock threat in his voice but also a solid note of steel ran through it.

"I do, indeed," she confirmed. "You listen to Clary and Brody. Do you hear me?"

He looked over at Clary and smiled. "Yeah. Well, if I don't listen to Clary, she'll knock me into tomorrow, and, if I'm not good, she won't bring me back, so no problem there."

At that, Brody burst out laughing. "Wow, she's already got you wrapped around her little finger, doesn't she?"

"She didn't need to," Larry disagreed. "One doesn't wrap angels around their fingers. One complies with their every wish." He walked over and gave Clary a big hug. "Thank you so much for doing all you can to keep me alive, yet again. I promise that, when I'm old enough and get a chance, I will do something to give back to this world in some way, to make up for all the time and effort you've put into me."

"Sweetie, listen to me," Clary replied, tapping his nose gently, her arm around his shoulders. "You are and always will be special, and what I do, that time and effort, I've done it out of love, so don't feel like you owe anybody." Larry gave her a misty smile.

Blair had tears starting to tickle down the back of her throat. She swallowed and turned to face Legend. "We've got two days. They'll stay here after we go, just long enough to get picked up by someone Terkel is sending over, although I don't really understand who he's sending."

"I'm pretty sure we have somebody not very far away," Brody noted, as he dropped his bag at the front door too.

"And not a minute too soon," he said, looking over at Clary. "You ready to go?"

She nodded. "There's still one cup of coffee left. I'll drink that." They watched as she got up, poured it, and then sat back down again.

"We have that kind of time?" Brody asked her hesitantly.

"No, not at all, but I want the coffee."

He winced at that. "Okay then."

"Hey, Riff," Clary called out, and a startled noise came on the other side of the front door.

"God damn it, how do you always know? Damn it."

"Well, if you didn't make quite so much noise, it would be a little harder."

He snorted at that. "Like hell. I was super quiet."

"Doesn't matter," Clary noted. "You make the air move."

At that, the newcomer stepped through the door into the living room and glared at her.

She just smiled at him benevolently. "So, you guys get everything loaded up, while I finish this coffee. Then we can go."

Riff frowned at her. "And you're sitting *and* drinking coffee while we do all the work, *huh*?" His tone confirmed he expected exactly that.

"Well, when you can tell when the air moves, you can be the last one to get loaded up. Right now, I'll have my coffee."

Such an inflexible note filled her tone that Riff looked over at Brody and raised an eyebrow.

Brody shook his head. "Yeah, let her have the coffee if she wants to." Then he turned, looked at Blair, and asked, "Are you sure about this?"

"You know I have to," she stated. "Even if all I do is confirm the one guy is Rip, that's important, and, if it's somebody else, we need to know who that player is too. I'm still the best chance we've got to ID these shadow players. Besides, it's not far away. Two days is our limit."

"Two days is *your* limit," Legend clarified, turning to look at her.

"I mean, until the job is done."

LEGEND LED THE way on foot through the bush, until they hit the main road. Blair didn't say anything but followed along at his side. He didn't know if she would read his mind—which was a very disconcerting thought, plus a reminder to keep his thoughts turned down to himself.

As they hit the main road, she still didn't say anything, just shouldered her pack and kept on going beside him.

"You really care about my brother, don't you?"

"I've looked after him for a long time," she stated quietly, "so, yes."

He just nodded.

"When the time is right, I'll leave him without any problem, not to worry," she stated, with a wry tone. "But you don't look after somebody who's been close to death like Larry has been and not become emotionally attached."

"No, I guess not. I can't even imagine what it would have been like, watching him fight for his life like he did."

"Exactly," she stated.

When a vehicle pulled up beside them, Riff got out. He never said a word, just turned and walked toward the cabin. She looked over at Legend. "Does he ever talk?"

"Not often, not to me at least. He talked to Clary though, and that's the only time I've ever witnessed him speaking."

Blair just nodded. At that she heard a second vehicle approaching, another AGV she presumed, and turned to see Brody and his team leaving in that one. "Interesting way you guys operate."

"Hey, I'm not even sure how this works, and Riff is fairly new to their team too, as I understand."

"Still not exactly a die-hard fan apparently," she murmured. "Or he's got some sort of agenda of his own."

"Everybody does. Everybody went into this line of business for a reason," he shared, "and generally we don't like people getting in our way." With that, he shot her a look, as if hoping she'd heard the rebuke for herself.

She just gave him a sunny smile and continued looking ahead.

"You never let things get to you, do you?" Legend muttered.

"If you're expecting me to back off because you're unhappy, too damn bad."

He groaned. "I can't keep you safe while I find out what I need to find out."

"If that were the truth, you would have fought harder to discourage me from tagging along," she argued, "and you didn't, so I took that as a yes."

He stopped as they got into the vehicle and looked at her. "Seriously?"

"Sure, if you actually cared and really said something about it, it would have made a difference in the way you replied," she stated, "but it didn't."

"So, you also knew I could cut down some of the travel

time and eliminate the time guarding you."

"Look. Let's just get this job done, and then we can get back over to *Cambridge*," she said, with an odd tone of voice.

He pulled out onto the road. "What about Cambridge?"

"I just never really thought that's where I'd end up."

He looked at her and frowned.

She sighed. "That's where Terkel's headquarters is."

"Right, I remember something about that." He drove carefully, his thoughts in a turmoil over her words. "Why do you think you'll end up there?"

She shrugged. "Pretty sure I can probably get a job with Terkel after this."

"You won't leave my brother, will you?" he asked, glancing at her.

"I said I wouldn't, but, at the moment, I'm not sure what that'll look like," she admitted, "and I really want to learn more about this energy work, if I can learn more."

He nodded. "You already have a lot of skills. I'm sure they could use whatever you can do."

"I don't really even know what I can do," she admitted bluntly. "I mean, how many times do you actually get a chance to turn around and say, *Hey, I can do this!*"

He burst out laughing, and she looked at him in surprise. He nodded. "I was just thinking that myself, you know? Then I imagine Terkel's team stepping out and saying, *Nice to know you want to join our team, but what is it you can do?* Yet I don't have any answers for them. It's not as if I've had any formal training and a certification from Psychics R Us or something."

She giggled at that. "Right? We're oddities in this world, and just knowing about Terk's place, where acceptance for this aspect of our world can be found, is a beautiful thought.

I really want to be part of it."

"In other words, you don't want to stick around and look after my brother for too long."

"No, I'm not saying that, but I do want to know more about what Terkel's team can do and what else I can learn to do. If I've learned anything from all of this, it's that, although I have some skills, I don't have nearly enough."

"I don't think anybody has enough," Legend replied, his tone harsh, even though he did his best to modulate it down. "Particularly while we're trying to protect somebody under attack. Whoever these assholes are, and whatever they're up to, the last thing we want is to have them succeed because we weren't good enough."

"I'm glad you agree," she replied quietly, as she looked over at him. "So, while you're gone doing whatever other missions you're planning on doing, I'm hoping to at least stay in touch with Terkel's team and see if I can do anything to help. And, if that has to be on a volunteer basis until I'm good enough to have something to offer, so be it."

He looked at her, startled. "You seriously don't think you have something to offer?"

"I don't know," she muttered. "Terkel, … what I have heard about him, sounds intimidating."

"I don't know about that," Legend disagreed. "I've heard that he's fair, but he doesn't necessarily suffer fools easily."

She burst out laughing at that. "I'm not sure anybody on Terk's team does," she noted. "Based on what I have heard and seen of Brody and you, seems a whole legion of men like you guys live and breathe," she shared, "and I would kind of like to meet them."

Legend felt a flash of anger that was almost jealousy slide through him, and he shot her a hard look. "Why?" he snapped. "You think your abilities will grow by sleeping with them?"

She stared at him, but her voice was calmer than it should have been, considering his rude remark. "No, I hadn't really considered that, but, now that you've brought it up, maybe I should give it a go." He continued to glare at her, and she laughed. "One of these days you'll admit what's between us."

"There's nothing between us," he stated immediately.

"Yeah, only because you keep the walls up," she pointed out. "I knew years ago, when I first met you, but you, on the other hand, are just plain stubborn."

He snorted. "There's also such a thing as a time and a place, and I haven't gotten to either. It also doesn't mean that, when I get to that time and place, you're it."

"Ouch." She winced. "Good to know that you can snap and play hardball like you do."

"Why?" he asked worriedly.

"Because now I'll feel completely comfortable snapping right back," she muttered and turned to the window. "Now drive, so we can get back faster, and shut up for the rest of the trip. After all, if I sleep with any men, I now know you can have nothing to say about it."

CHAPTER 12

SEVERAL HOURS LATER Blair clued into where they were going. She looked over at him. "Are we going back to the mansion?" she asked in disbelief. He gave a clipped nod. "But why?"

"Because paperwork and laptops and things are there that we need for Larry's future," Legend replied.

"The paperwork should all be online, and his manager should have it—or at least the estate lawyer and the accountants will."

"Yeah, and what they'll provide versus what actually is there is probably a whole different story."

"Two sets of books? Of course." She sank back into the front seat and pondered that. "The mansion is likely to be overrun at this point."

"There is a chance of that, but I'm also hoping and half expecting it to be overrun or to maybe find a theft in progress, by whoever set this up. A lot of lootable valuables are in that house."

"Yes, but the house itself is what's truly valuable."

He nodded again. "I agree, but, if we're trying to find out who's behind this, that's the best place to start. There has to be a clue."

"It's also suicide," she noted.

He glanced at her, flashed a grin, and asked, "Still want

to come? I can drop you off, and you can go back to the cabin at any time."

She jutted her chin out at him and glared.

He shrugged. "Just an idea."

"Yeah, well, it's not a good idea," she snapped. "If you're determined to do this, then so am I."

"Yeah, and what is your reasoning behind that?" he asked curiously. "I'm trying to make sure we don't have any more attacks, and, for that, I need to get as much information from his mansion as I can. If I can snag laptops and things, I will."

"I want Larry to be safe, so that is my reason. So don't you think we should have searched the mansion for that stuff in the first place then?"

He shrugged. "Yeah, that would have been nice, but I don't recall having any extra time when we took off out of there before we heard gunshots. Now, I don't know if anybody has even made a move on the place, though I certainly would have. Plus, if I hadn't had so many people to look after when first escaping the mansion, I would have been back there in a heartbeat," he explained.

"It's not as if we're that far away."

"No, but we're just far enough away that we aren't around the corner."

"I saw that, and I'll put it down to the fact that I was sleeping for not having noticed earlier."

"Well, if you'd asked me ahead of time, I could have told you where we were headed, but you didn't. You were too hell-bent on coming with me."

"Sure, and maybe if I had understood why we were coming here, I wouldn't have been so shocked."

He shrugged. "Sorry, not used to explaining myself."

"Well, you might want to consider getting into the habit of it," she snapped, then sagged in place. "It doesn't make any difference. We're here now."

"Exactly," he said cheerfully, "and you need to stay close. I'm not sure what we'll find, if anything, but I need to snag as much as I can."

"What about the vehicle?"

"We'll park in the back acreage, then go in cross-country."

"Are you really expecting anybody to be there?"

"I had Terkel scout it out, and people have been back and forth. He didn't say anything about permanent lodgers or at least nothing that looked as if anybody was staying to that extent."

"Interesting," she murmured. "But then, it's not really the place that Mr. Kartal stayed at all the time, is it?"

"No, but it is one of his favorite homes, and he did a lot of work there."

She pondered that. "He has a safe in his home office too." He seemed surprised. She shrugged and added, "Hey, everybody ignores the hired help."

He laughed. "That's the last thing you were."

"To your father, I was," she stated. "He never saw me, never understood anything about me, and never cared to."

"Well, don't take it personally. He didn't care to know anything about anybody, including his own kids."

"Right, and I probably should be grateful that he ignored me all the time. As long as I kept Larry occupied and his schooling going forward, I was doing my job, and Mr. Kartal didn't care to know about anything else."

"Did you ever go to him with problems?"

"God no," she replied. "He didn't want to know about

anything like that. Problems meant we weren't all doing our jobs."

He laughed at that. "Yeah, if only life were that simple."

"Well, for him, it apparently was."

"Well, it's definitely not that simple now."

"Do we really think he's dead?" When he frowned at her, she shrugged. "I don't know why it's bugging me. It's just … you know? For all we know, that was just a media story. I feel like he's gone, but we haven't had a solid confirmation."

"That's a good point too," Legend agreed. "I did consider it, but, until we actually get confirmation, what is it you want me to say?"

"I guess you don't know either," she said. "I keep expecting that you'll have answers, but you won't have any more than I do. I just thought you would have doubts."

"Hopefully we'll know more soon. I can get a few more answers maybe, but we'll still have to wait for some final confirmation, since we didn't actually see his body ourselves."

"Which we didn't, but it would make sense that Mr. Kartal would attempt to do something like that, faking his death, in order to get out of the trouble he is in."

"I wouldn't be at all surprised," Legend agreed, with a nod. "That doesn't make me feel any better though."

At that, she nodded. "He always was kind of slippery." Legend didn't say anything to that, and when they pulled into the shrubs at the back of the property, she hopped out, looked around, and asked, "Is this really adjacent to the mansion?"

"It is, but it's another mile cross-country."

"Well, if we have an awful lot to carry back, that won't

be very easy to do," she noted, contemplating the distance.

"Carry what you can. I'll take the rest," he replied.

She looked over at him, registering the breadth of his shoulders and the power of his arms. "Yeah, you might as well just carry all of it," she muttered, "compared to what I'll carry."

He just nodded, as if fully accepting that was the way it was.

She sighed. "I'm not that weak, you know?"

"Hey, I didn't say a word," he pointed out cheerfully, "but you sure do complain a lot." She glared at him. His lips twitched, and he picked up what she now realized were several empty backpacks from the rear seat of the vehicle.

"Presumably to make life easy?"

He nodded. "Yeah, if we have a lot to carry, I need to carry it."

She noted he was bringing ropes with him too. "Well, give me something to take."

He pointed out two ropes in the back.

She quickly slung one over her shoulder and grabbed another one in her hand. Then seeing zap straps, she looked at him, shrugged, and grabbed them too. "Interesting choice."

"Hey, I like them."

"Why? Because they are hard to get out of?"

"I figured they might come in handy. And actually, they can be easy to get out of, but only if you know how, and so very often nobody knows how."

"Well then, you can show me how later," she stated. "Right now, it's more important that we use them on people who potentially might not know how."

"Yeah, but anybody in this field will get out of them

pretty fast," Legend added.

"Well, we have rope too."

"Agreed." With that, he moved some brush around to camouflage the vehicle ever-so-slightly.

"Does anybody even come back here? It looks like a completely deserted back road."

"Which just means that, given the circumstances, there'll be quite a bit of traffic."

Not a whole lot she could say to that, so she stepped behind him as he raced through the trees. Now that they were actually here, he was apparently in some sort of a rush. He'd driven hard and fast, but she had settled into the speed soon enough and had forgotten he was going as quickly as he was. Now that they were outside, running, it was a whole different story.

He glanced back at her. "If you can't keep up, go back to the car," he snapped.

"I'm keeping up," she replied, keeping her tone and her breathing even. "I just wasn't expecting an all-out run."

"Well, that's what it'll be until we can get the hell out of here," he noted. "If you can't do it, you know what the answer is."

"*Get lost*," she said, without rancor. "I'll keep up. Don't you worry about it." She felt his gaze assessing her intently, then he turned that laser focus back to their surroundings, as he maintained the same punishing pace. But she meant it that she would keep up, and, if they could find anything here to help Larry and could put a stop to this nightmare, she was all for it. She would play her part; she just hadn't anticipated having to do it at fifty miles an hour. An exaggeration, but damn.

It didn't take long for her muscles to start screaming, but

she knew the minute she wavered and let him know, he'd put a stop to her even having anything to do with him and this or any other missions, and that wouldn't work out so well for her. When he suddenly reached out a hand, and she slammed into it, she stopped and tried to get her breath back.

"Somebody's up ahead," he whispered, as he peered through the bushes.

She tried to peer through the bushes too but couldn't see anything. She had to trust that he knew what he was talking about. "Friend or foe?"

"At this point they're all foes," he muttered. "Treat everyone like an enemy."

She winced at that. "Unless I know them."

"Chances are, if you know them, they know you, and they'll know who's supposed to be with you," he pointed out, "so don't expect that to get you out of trouble."

"Right," she muttered.

When he gave the word, he said, "Now be quiet. We'll go in through the back door of the loading area."

She nodded, and, by the time they were inside the mansion, her breath was back to normal, and she watched through a window at a guy, talking on the phone at the far side of the property. "Do you think he saw us?"

"No, he sure didn't, but he is talking to somebody, and I wish I knew who it was."

"He's pretty relaxed though, isn't he?" she muttered, staring at his stance.

"Yeah, for the moment. Come on. We've got to go." And, with that, she followed him through the industrial kitchens to the main floor, where he stopped again and assessed the sounds.

She couldn't hear anything, and apparently he was of the same opinion, as he quickly led her upstairs toward the office. As they got closer, she stopped, listened, and shrugged. "Still sounds empty."

He nodded. "That's a good thing." In the office, he quickly went to the desk. It was locked, but it popped open in seconds, and he started sorting through the paperwork, looking for anything. She opened up a drawer on the far side and pulled out a laptop. He glanced at it and nodded. "We're taking that with us."

She nodded too. "It would help to have his log-ins."

"Not a problem really," he replied. "They'll have no problem getting into it back at Terkel's place."

She didn't say anything, wondering at a team who could get into laptops so easily, then realized that most people probably weren't aware that code breakers took lessons and, in a few hours, could get into almost anything. Hell, she wasn't even sure how she knew that, but it was something to do with questions Larry had asked her once. So she'd gone down the rabbit hole of research to find out. That was life with Larry, who was nothing if not inquisitive.

He had an inquiring mind, and she'd done her best to answer as many of his questions as she could. She knew her time for teaching him anything he didn't already know was potentially running out, but that wasn't the issue at hand. As she put the laptop inside the backpack, she found another tablet, some paperwork, and a stack of what looked like credit cards and bank cards. She held them up.

Legend looked at them briefly, then nodded. "Take them too."

She went through and grabbed anything that looked financial or business related. By the time Legend was done with his part of the desk, he had a backpack full too. She asked, "How come Mr. Kartal has so much of this stuff here?"

"Because he was involved in a lot," Legend muttered. "Yet there's no cash, and that surprises me."

"No, it's in that safe," she said, pointing to the wall. At his frown, she shrugged. "I told you. Nobody ever thinks about the help."

"You've actually been in here when it was open?"

"Yes, and he didn't even bother shutting it. Again I was nobody to him."

He nodded, then quickly looked back at her.

She added, "Behind the painting."

He lifted the painting off the wall, and there was a wall safe. "I don't suppose you know the code, do you?"

"No, and that would help, wouldn't it? Hang on a minute." She went back over to the desk and lifted the large desk pad. Underneath was a scratch pad filled with numbers. "I remember he had a habit of slipping things under here sometimes too." She studied the notes for a moment, then read off some numbers to him.

Legend smiled. "Yeah, that would make sense. It's Larry's birthday."

"Interesting," she muttered. "He must have been planning on changing it again."

"He changed it constantly, but it was variations of the same numbers, I think," Legend replied. Sure enough, the safe opened on his third attempt. Inside was paperwork, a lot of cash, and several weapons.

She stared at that and winced. "Do you think it's safe to take it all?"

"Yeah, better than letting the bad guys keep all this,"

Legend stated. Then he quickly unloaded the safe into his other backpack. Snatching up the weapons, he checked to see if they were already loaded, then slipped one into the back of his belt. With the safe emptied and now locked again, he put the picture back in place, did another quick circle around the office, and then stopped at the desk again. He ran his hands over a couple spots around the back, pressing at certain points.

"Did he have secret drawers?" she asked, her voice an excited whisper.

He nodded. "I know of at least two."

It took him ten minutes. She was constantly staring at the doorway, biting her bottom lip, until a drawer popped out. He smiled. It was full of golden bars, shimmering in the dim light. "Now that is gold." He nodded and quickly put everything into a smaller cloth bag, then put that bag into his jacket and zipped up the pocket. Then he went to the next secret drawer and quickly got it open. She wasn't even sure what was in there, but he stared at it, swore, then snatched it up and quickly put it into his last backpack. "Now we're getting the hell out of here."

"Then what?"

"Don't worry about it," he said. "First we get out of here and get this all safe and away from these morons."

"What about the guy who put out the contract?"

"We'll be on that next, so let's go." And, with that, he quickly raced through the hallway, back down the way they came. As she went around the corner behind him, she heard a shout, and Legend swore. "Sorry," she said. "I guess I was just a little too slow taking that last corner."

"No, I was expecting somebody," he noted.

With that, racing footsteps could be heard behind them

and somebody yelling, "Stop or I'll shoot."

She bent down low, expecting to feel a bullet any second, but Legend quickly pulled her around the next corner and waited. They were just a hair from being outside. Escape was tantalizing and close.

Then he whispered, "Don't even think about it."

She glared at him, but he just smiled as the person chasing them came around the corner, hell-bent at a horrifying speed. Legend stuck out a foot, tripping him up. He went flying, the gun slipping from his hand and skittering across the floor. Just like that, Legend was on him. After two hard blows to the jaw, he was out cold.

Blair frowned, went over, and took a look. "It's one of the security guards," she said in surprise.

Legend quickly pulled out the guy's ID, looked it over, then took several photos of it and him, sending them off to somebody, presumably Terkel. "Come on. Let's go." Legend took his IDs but left the man on the ground to wake up at his leisure, assuming that he'd somehow been attacked or just plain tripped. Once outside, unwilling to give her any relief, he kept pushing her to move faster and faster. At this point, she was flat-out running, knowing they were up against any number of other security guards on the place. Even if it wasn't the security guards, it could be any number of other armed people. By the time he got her to the vehicle, she could hardly breathe.

He pulled away the brush, opened up the car, urgently motioned for her to get in.

She looked over at him and asked, "You think he wasn't alone?"

"I know he wasn't alone," he stated, as he quickly got into the vehicle and started it up. Pulling out at top speed, he was soon out of the shrubbery and onto the road, headed back the way they came. Almost instantly shots were fired in their direction. She shrieked and crouched down low.

"Stay down," he snapped. "I don't know how quickly they'll come after us, but you can bet they're on their way."

"Why?" she asked, then realized what a stupid question it was. He just glanced at her once, and she nodded. "You're right, stupid question."

He laughed, his tone bright and cheerful, as if it were an everyday thing.

She stared at him. "Have you lost your mind?"

"Nah."

"You really love this kind of stuff, don't you?"

"Not necessarily, but there's a certain adrenaline rush that comes from succeeding."

"Do you think we succeeded?" she asked drily.

"Well, we've taken quite a haul out of there, so, if my father is alive, he'll be pissed and looking for all that shit back. If he's not alive, it's definitely something I don't want other people to get their hands on."

"Good point," she agreed, "but we're still not any closer to finding out who put out the contract, and, if it was Richard, we need to contact him and get this to stop."

"Yeah, but hopefully now we'll have a hell of a lot more information to work with," Legend pointed out. When they quickly hit more traffic, he slowed down to just barely above the speed limit.

"The last thing we want is to get pulled over," she cautioned him, watching the speedometer at a crazy pace.

"Yeah, I know, but I'm pretty-damn sure we'll have somebody coming up behind us pretty soon."

And, with that, he quickly made several changes in direction and zipped from corner to corner, block to block, until she was almost dizzy with it. "Aren't we out of danger yet?" she asked, when he finally straightened his course and coasted forward.

"I think so, but we need to change vehicles fast."

He pulled into a parking lot and drove around to the back. He found a hatchback there, kind of beat-up and older, probably belonging to one of the employees. He got out, quickly hot-wired it, then moved her and their gear over. Moments later, he shot out of the parking lot.

"Damn, I feel bad about the person we just took this from."

"Well, it's insured, and he'll probably get far more money out of that than what this thing is worth. This is on its last legs."

"Won't they wonder why anybody would steal it?" she muttered.

"Yeah, and that is also why they won't be looking for us in a car like this."

She pondered that strange logic, as he drove in a direction she hadn't really expected. "Where are we now?" she asked in exasperation.

"No clue," Legend admitted, "but, as long as we keep going away from where we need to be, we're better off."

"And, of course, we don't want to be anywhere close to where they're expecting us to be."

"That's true enough."

"What we should be doing is heading back to England, but we can't because we haven't found anything," she muttered.

"Well, we found a bit of stuff, but now we need to grab a motel room just for a couple hours to look at it better. I want to go over this information and see if we can get an idea of what's really going on. We have a good idea, but let's get down to the bottom of it for sure." Just then his phone rang. He pulled it from his pocket and barked into the phone. "Yeah, what's up?"

At first came silence on the other end. "Was that you?" asked a man, his tone hard.

Legend stared at the phone. "Was that me where?"

"At the house."

"Who is this?" he asked.

"Somebody who wants that money bad."

"What money?"

"The money from the safe you just wiped out."

"Oh, that's interesting," Legend replied. "Now that you mention it, anything at the house would belong to Larry."

"He doesn't need anything," the man on the other end stated in exasperation. "He's just a kid."

"He's a kid, but he also needs to grow up and to get an education. Right now, depending on what becomes of the estate of his father, that'll be even harder for him to do."

"His dad is dead," the man stated with harsh clarity. "*Your* dad. Do you think I don't know who you are? I caught sight of you racing through the trees with some chick. What kind of an idiot have you turned out to be that you actually take a woman on a trip like this?"

"When the woman is just too ornery to stay behind," he replied, with a half laugh. "I don't know who the hell this is, so you need to talk to me. Why not introduce yourself?"

"You need to talk to me because I know exactly where that kid brother of yours is, and I'll take him out if you don't bring me back the contents of that safe."

"That's interesting because the contents of that safe

weren't enough to write home about. Just enough to give the kid an education and some sense of a normal life."

"So *you* say," he snapped, and his tone turned ugly. "Your father left behind a hell of a lot of stuff worth stealing."

"Well, we'll see about that," Legend replied. "I don't even know what he left behind, but what I do know is that the government will likely confiscate most of it."

"Yeah, but I'm not into lifting the family silver. I want an awful lot of blackmail material and some really good leverage on people. You give me all that, and I'll leave your brother alone."

"If I don't?"

"Your brother is marked," he declared.

"Seems he already is. Are you the one who put out the contract on him already?" Legend asked, his voice calm, as he searched the area around them. Up ahead was a motel. He quickly pulled into the parking lot, shut off the engine, and said, "We need to meet."

"Yeah, we sure do. You give me what I want, and I'll give you what you want."

"Yeah? And how will you pull that contract if you're not the one who actually posted it?"

He hesitated and then added, "Richard posted it. I can get him to pull it."

"Sure, you say that, but Richard must have a reason for it."

"Yeah, because everything goes to your brother, so whoever controls him controls the money."

"That's nice, but that also means that I have to die first."

At that came an ugly laugh on the other end. "I wondered if you had figured that out. You've been kind of slow up until now."

"Oh, I'm not slow at all," Legend declared. "I'm the guardian, and I intend to stay that way. Should anything happen to me, the money is going into a very well-run charity fund."

"*Charity*," he repeated, aghast.

"Charity. So, if anybody takes me out, it won't make a damn bit of difference. So, spread the word. There's no money for anyone. If it's not Larry's, then it goes to charity. Every bit."

"God damn it. No way you've had a chance to work any of that yet."

"Yeah, I sure have. I'm just waiting for the final paperwork now. I just have to lay low until it's signed, and, if you take me out after that, it won't make a damn bit of difference."

"Yeah, but all the assets have to get moved first. There's paperwork involved, and it takes time."

"Yeah, well, we heard about my father's death yesterday, so believe me. That paperwork is well and truly taken care of."

At that, the other man swore. "I still want the contents of that backpack you ran out of here with."

"You can't have the backpack," Legend stated. "Besides, you told me that you wanted the contents of the safe."

At that, the other guy asked, "What else did you get?"

"None of your business. It's all for my brother." It was obvious that the guy didn't believe him. "You tell Richard that I want to meet with him and that I want to put an end to this."

"Well, he'll want money for that, and big money, because your brother is worth big money."

"No, he isn't. That's been taken off the table, and tell him I'm off the table as well. He won't get any money out of it."

"He'll put you back on the table just for fun," he said, with a laugh. "You know that."

"Yeah, I do know that. He also knows that I play hardball. Tell him to call me. I'll be looking forward to it." With that, Legend ended the call.

LEGEND PAID FOR a room with cash under an alias. Then returned to Blair, opened the car door, and said, "Come on. We're going upstairs." He quickly grabbed the bags and nudged Blair ahead of him into the second-floor room.

As soon as the door was closed, she turned and asked him, "Now what?"

He walked to the nearest bed and dropped the bags there. "We need to get through as much of this information as we can to figure out what we're up against, and then I need to set up a meeting with Richard." When she just nodded, he looked over at her with a frown. "Are you okay?" he asked. She just nodded again, and he glared at her. "Hey, I didn't want you to come. Remember?"

"I'm stubborn. Remember?"

Just something about her poked at his sense of humor, and he laughed. "Isn't that the truth," he muttered. "It could be the end of you one day."

"It just might be," she agreed cheerfully. "It really brings home the games that your dad played and how dangerous they were."

"They were always dangerous. It was always a game to

him, and he didn't give a damn who got hurt in the process."

"You must have really hated him."

He stopped to consider that, then faced her. "You know that *hate* is a hard word when it comes to family," he began, looking away from her now. "Not just a hard word but it's even difficult to justify that kind of emotion for a man like my father, who was essentially devoid of emotions, at least the healthy kinds. He was a user. He didn't love my mother, and he didn't love Larry's mother. It was all about what they could do for him. In my mother's case, it was five minutes of pleasure and then he was done, and he left her with a lifetime of child-rearing and never looked back."

"Wow, that doesn't sound great."

"No, it sure wasn't. Larry's mother was no different, except my father decided that having a wealthy, well-connected wife would do more for his career than somebody *cheap and easy, like my mother*. His words, not mine."

Blair winced.

"No, I don't give a damn about my father's words, and any insults against my mother have absolutely no bearing on my reality, not back then and not now. She's been dead and gone a long time, and her life was absolute shit because of him, but I'm not getting into that with him or with anybody else. I loved her dearly, but I didn't have a whole lot to do with her either. She chose drugs after him, and it was a downward slide from there. I'm not telling you all this for sympathy. I just want you to know that all that family stuff really doesn't have anything to do with me."

"I think it does," she disagreed, "but you just don't want to admit it."

He rolled his eyes at that. "Whatever." He quickly unpacked the stuff they had taken from his father's office and the safe.

"That's a lot of money," she stated, realizing it for the first time.

"It is, but I don't know that it's nearly enough for these guys to actually back off and to get out of our lives."

"Will you try to buy them off?"

"No, because, if they think we have this much, they'll assume we have access to a lot more." He sat on the bed, gripping his head in his hands for a second. He looked exhausted. "The minute you start paying for something like this, all hell breaks loose, and they keep coming back."

She looked at the money and nodded. "I think we should pack all this up, so it's ready to go in a heartbeat."

"Absolutely. Can you do that? I need to get the laptops out and start sorting through what's in these computer files." With that, he opened up his laptop and started popping in the USB keys, also taken from the safe. She packed up the money and the jewels that were in the safe.

She hadn't even realized he had grabbed any, but he'd just cleaned it all out, not caring what was there. There were also some papers. She went through the small stack and found Larry's birth certificate, as well as the marriage certificate. It was a business arrangement. She winced as she read the terms and agreement. Larry's mother was supposed to get five million dollars after the birth of her son, as long as she stayed long enough for Mr. Kartal to get elected. Instead he'd obviously killed her or she passed away on her own, when Larry was just a couple of years old.

Blair took several photos of everything she'd found, put the paperwork back together, and finished loading up the bag, putting it behind the door so it was ready to go. Then she moved over next to Legend, where he was staring at the computer. "Well?"

"Blackmail," he said, his voice thick with anger. "Blackmail photos on other politicians, families, anything he could use to force people to do what he wanted them to do. Take bribes, send legislation through. It's all here," he muttered. "I've only been through three keys so far. Damn him anyway."

"This isn't really anything new for you though, is it?"

"No, I already knew he was a bastard," Legend stated, standing up and glaring at her. "But it's one thing to know, and it's another thing to see it in black and white like this."

She nodded. "Are you making copies of everything?"

He hesitated and then nodded. "I am. I just don't know why."

"Well, at least if we lose everything in the bags, we'll have digital copies of the documents, of the data on the USBs, in case we need it again," she murmured. "We don't really know how bad this can get."

With a nod, he quickly went through the rest of the keys. As she sat and watched him go through a couple of them, she realized she really didn't want to know anymore because these were people's secrets, sordid details, love affairs, some thefts, and definitely some crooked deals.

By the time he was done, and everything had been copied over, he looked down at the USB keys and declared, "These are definitely bargaining chip material."

"It is, but what about all these people?"

"I think they've probably already been set up as much as they can be," he muttered, "but I could be wrong."

"Do they ever get to have peace and quiet after this? This will be something they're tormented by forever."

"Good point," he replied, looking over at her, half smiling. "And you want me to destroy it all."

"I don't know what I want to do right now," she admitted. "As much as I do want to think that this won't be an issue, I also want to ensure we have a way to get Larry a safe life again."

He nodded, and started going through some other files found on the office laptop. "I've copied over as much of this as I can." Then he put all of the USB keys into a pile on the bed. "There's still way more stuff to go through on this laptop too." He looked over at her. "What did you find in the safe?"

She quickly gave him a rundown and added, "I took photos of them all, even the birth certificate and the marriage contract for Larry's sake."

"Right, just what he really needs to know, isn't it?"

She nodded. "Maybe later, when he's an adult, it will be something he should be aware of. I don't know, but, if we lose it, then there's no record of it."

"Right," Legend agreed. "I'll go through some of these, and then we need food and a bit of rest. Thereafter, hopefully we're getting on the road again."

"Where are we going then?"

"You'll stay here, and I'll go meet Richard."

"Do you really think it'll be that easy?"

"No, I don't think it'll be easy at all," he muttered. "He'll set me up and try to take me down, and, beyond that, I have no idea."

"Do you think he has any plans to let you go free?"

He looked over at her with a wry smile. "Would you?"

"Yes, actually I would." She gave a half laugh. "That doesn't mean he will."

LEGEND LOOKED OVER at Blair, as they ate several granola bars, which was all the food they had. The motel had a coffee vending machine, which they'd both delicately tasted and then immediately dumped.

She asked, "I guess there's no hope of getting some real food, is there?"

"Not right now," he said, just as his phone rang. He looked down at it, then frowned. "Hey, Terkel." He put it on Speaker, and Terk's voice filled the room.

"It's a trap, you know."

"Well, I haven't gotten any communication yet to say whether it's even on or not," he replied in a mild tone. "We can definitely expect it to be a trap, but I still feel as if I need to meet him."

"Meet him or take him out?" Terkel's voice was calm, as if interested, but not bothered either way. But surely he heard the audible gasp from Blair.

Legend shook his head. "Whichever way this guy wants it to play out," he declared, his voice hard. "We both know this has to stop one way or another."

"Absolutely," Terkel agreed, "but you haven't actually spoken to this Richard yet, have you?"

"No, just the one guy who wanted his stuff back. I told you about that conversation."

"Yes, you did. Oh, by the way, Brody and Clary arrived. Larry is here, safe and sound."

"Oh, thank God for that," Blair said, racing closer to the phone. "How is he holding up?"

"He's actually in very good spirits. He's pretty over-whelmed with joy about the castle."

"Castle?"

First came silence, then Terkel laughed. "Yes, our place here is actually a castle."

"Oh, wow," Blair exclaimed, "like that alone won't make everybody come running."

"Well, it's not intended for *everybody* to come running," he replied, with a note of humor, "but it does seem to bring out the interest factor."

"Yeah, you're not kidding," she muttered. "Well, as long as he made it there safe." Then she looked over at Legend. "Legend is pretty determined to go on this adventure alone."

"Of course he is, and that's another reason I'm calling."

"Okay," Legend replied. "What's up?"

"Riff is still over there, so he's coming as backup."

"Oh." Legend had an odd note in his tone. "I guess that's probably a good idea."

"What?" she cried out. "It's a good idea for Riff to come, but not me?" He shot her a look. "So what if he knows what he's doing," she muttered. "It still doesn't change the fact that you won't know who you're dealing with."

"But we're not certain that you know this guy either," Legend pointed out.

She nodded, then shrugged. "I do seem to be in the way more than I'm helpful."

"That's not true." He turned his attention back to Terk on the phone. "I emailed a lot of stuff to you, copies of materials that we found at the mansion."

"I went through some of it," Terkel noted, his voice deepening. "Lots of nastiness on that."

"Yeah, I'm pretty sure my father was using it to get what he wanted. I have a lot of documents I still haven't seen, plus a lot of information on credit cards, bank accounts, statements, and that kind of thing. I've taken photos, and I'll send them to you tonight," he added. "Maybe we can track some of the bank accounts for Larry's sake. Also, quite a bit of cash is here."

"If you need to use the cash to buy Larry's freedom …" Blair began.

"Think that through," Terkel said. "As soon as they know there is that kind of cash, they'll want more."

"That's what I told her," Legend stated.

"Is everybody so greedy?" she asked bitterly.

Legend grabbed her hand and squeezed it gently. "Most of the time they are, and, in this mess, these guys are scared. Their leader's down. Their plans went awry, and now they're all trying to scramble for survival. That's all anybody cares about right now, and, if we understand that and realize these guys are dangerous because they're cornered and can't even get out of town, hopefully it will keep us all alive."

"Not really," she argued, the stress and worry clearly taking a toll. "If he thinks you've got the money, then what's to stop him from just shooting you dead on sight?"

He winced. "I was kind of hoping they wouldn't do that," he quipped, a laugh in his voice.

She glared at him. "It's hardly a laughing matter."

"I told you to stay with Larry and the others."

"Yeah. Well, I didn't," she muttered. "Believe me. You're beginning to make me wish I had."

He groaned. "I don't think Terk needs to listen to us squabbling."

"No, but it's more interesting than anything I had going on here," Terk added, with a note of humor. "You guys do need to get your relationship between yourselves settled. It'll make it a lot easier if you do it before you get here and find yourselves doing it in front of everybody."

At that, she stopped, stared, and asked, "Meaning?"

"You know perfectly well what I mean," he said in a gentler tone. "It's one thing to have a family dispute on your own," Terk added, "but in a place like this? Everybody'll know, and more than that, they'll know what the details are too. We do our best to keep to ourselves, but it isn't something that happens easily."

She winced, as she looked over at Legend. "Well, thanks for the warning," she muttered.

"You know perfectly well what it's like when you're around other psychics. When you were with Clary or close to Clary, your own abilities increased, did they not?"

"Yes, but I wasn't sure whether it was because of her or not."

"Yeah, and Brody, plus Legend, have their own skills of course. Skills that I'm still hoping Legend will put to use here with our team."

"I don't know that he's all that cooperative," she shared. "He can be difficult."

At that, Legend sighed. "Hey, I'm still here. Terk, we'll talk later." Moments later, his phone rang again. He quickly answered with a bark to his tone.

"You want to meet. I want to meet," a stranger said on the phone. "I'm half an hour away. Leave the lady behind."

"She doesn't want to be left behind," Blair stated in a snappy voice. "She wants Larry safe."

At that, the stranger laughed. "Larry has definitely earned himself some saviors," he noted, "which I find very interesting. Now why would anybody give a damn, I wonder."

"No need to overwork your brain," she declared, her

voice darkening. "It would be enough to know that we care about people."

"Caring about people will get you killed, so, if you haven't learned that by now, come at your own peril. You damn-well better bring all that cash and preferably any other paperwork you stole from the house. There's money to be had by all, but I am determined to get my share. I've put a lot of years into this cause, his cause, and I'm not walking away with nothing." And, with that, he seemingly disconnected.

"But wait, where are we meeting?" she asked the void.

The stranger laughed. "Legend knows."

After that came only silence.

CHAPTER 13

"WHERE?" BLAIR DEMANDED.

Legend sighed. "Back at the mansion."

"Oh, no, that's not a good idea. It's really hard to get out of that place."

"We've managed to do it twice now," he reminded her.

"I know, but still, who says there will be a third successful escape?" She hated the idea, and she was having absolutely no luck in changing his mind.

"I think you should stay here."

"Only to spend the rest of my life waiting for you to return?" she muttered. "Hell no."

"At least that way, if I don't come back, you'll know perfectly well where you can go. Head over to Terk's and look after Larry, and use all the money we got to try and get him to adulthood, so he can have a decent life," Legend told her, his voice rough. "I'm leaving you the cash and everything we got."

She glared at him.

"Look. I'm not taking you. It's too dangerous. I'll have Riff as backup, and that's as good as it'll get."

She stared at him, feeling the same anger but more than that now. Fear washed all over her.

He frowned at her. "You really don't think I'll come back, do you?"

She swallowed hard. "I'm afraid you won't come back," she clarified. "There's a difference."

"That's true, but it's not one I'm prepared to argue over."

She groaned. "He's not planning on letting you free."

"Maybe not, but I'm not planning on letting him live either," he replied.

She shook her head, glaring at him. "He'll already be in position, with who-knows-how-many traps set up. If you even try to go in the same way, you know you'll be taken immediately."

"Hopefully Riff has some ideas about that or will already be in position himself." At that, he tilted his head to the side.

She frowned. "What's that?" she asked.

"Terk is talking to me."

Her gaze widened. "The fact that he can even do that is amazing."

"He can do a lot more, but it's much easier if he has the ability to focus on just me and not you."

She glared at him. "Oh, so now you're telling me that I'm in the way."

"Of course you're in the way, and, worse than that, you'll be used as leverage, and that's the last thing I want. They are threatening Larry's life, but if they got ahold of you ..." His words trailed off, turning rough. "Look. I don't want to see you hurt, and I certainly don't want to be in a position where I'm giving up secrets or my brother in exchange for you," he admitted, still glaring at her.

She could see the emotions in his gaze.

"You need to stay here," he repeated. "You need to stay out of trouble."

She studied him for a moment, unsure how to break

through that resistance, until she realized there really wasn't any way to get through it. He was adamant. "Fine," she muttered. "In that case, I might as well pack up and head over to Terkel's then."

"Well, you don't have to be quite so fatalistic," Legend replied, with a note of humor. "A little more faith would help."

"Would it though?" she asked, turning to look at him. "It seems more like fantasy."

"Sometimes we need that too." He ran his hand through his hair, as he slowly turned and took stock of things here. "What I really need is to know that I don't have to worry about you, so I can focus on what I need to do at the mansion," he shared. "And remember. *This* is the work I do."

She nodded, but her throat was tight. "I hear you. I still think it sucks though."

He smiled. "Lots of things in life suck."

"Yeah, but you don't have to give your life for them."

He stiffened, then turned and glared at her. "I'm coming back," he snapped. "Do you want to stop putting that thought out there?"

She raised both hands, then walked over to the other bed and threw herself down on top of the covers. "Fine," she muttered, "if you say so." She stared up at the ceiling, knowing she wasn't acting very well, but the fear was choking her deep inside, and there wasn't anything she could think of to make it any better. "You need to look at this from a rational point of view though," she added, "since he is out there to try and kill you."

"Yes, I know that," he stated, with exaggerated patience. "We've already ascertained that he'll try whatever he can to take me down."

"Yeah, we did. But what will you do to ensure that doesn't happen?" she asked, turning to look at him.

He stopped and stared. "Well, Riff will be a big help, and, with any luck, I can maybe use Terkel or some of these hidden weapons that they all seem to have," he muttered.

"And if that doesn't work?"

"Well, I have the same old set of skills I've always had, my own, which have served me pretty well over the years," he muttered. "And a little bit of faith on your part would help."

"I know that you'll do the best you can," she conceded, "but this guy won't give a shit. Plus, if you don't go with a backpack, making it look like you have a lot, you know that somebody will be backtracking you."

"Good point," he muttered. "We need to change your room here, so nobody can find you." With that, he got up and walked out of the motel room.

She got to her feet. That's not what she had expected out of him, but it did make sense because, if anybody was keeping an eye on him, his vehicle, or had some way to track the energy, then she wouldn't be safe here.

Honestly the thought of being left here alone without him to protect her also made her feel that she was one step away from death herself, and it wouldn't be a nice death. She winced at all these errant thoughts, and, when he finally returned, she glared at him. "And?"

"I think a better place for you is about two doors down," he whispered, turning to look back outside. "It's empty, and I've just picked the lock so you can get in. If you stay inside, nobody will know you are there, so you should be safe until I get back."

She nodded. "You do know that I'll track you."

He stopped, turned, and then frowned at her. "What?"

Such a low and deadly tone filled his voice that she stared at him. "I'll track you," she repeated defiantly.

"As in … how?"

"Ah." She shrugged. "The same way I track Larry, whenever he goes off and does his disappearing act."

"He does a disappearing act?"

"Well, he did, until he realized it didn't work. I learned it while he was so ill. It was something that Clary taught me to do, way back when."

"You track him?"

"I track him on the ethers. Whenever he got to the point of having these relapses, I would connect with Clary and, with her help, we would bring him back again. I don't know how to explain it better than that. I've never tried to do it with anybody else, but I'll do it with you."

"What do you think that will do?" he asked her curiously. "I mean, even if you could track me, what difference does it make?"

She pondered that, shrugged, and admitted, "I don't know, but I guess it feels like the one thing I can do, … so I'll do it for me."

"That's fine. I don't have a problem with you tracking me, as long as you have no way to interfere when things are happening. You don't, do you?"

"I don't think so," she replied, "but I wish I did."

He smiled at that. "We'll have to talk about tracking afterward."

She shrugged. "Well, it's not as if you talk about any of your abilities."

"Who says I even have any?"

"Why would Terkel want you if you didn't have any?"

Legend burst out laughing at that. "Good point. Let's grab the bags and get you situated."

They quickly grabbed everything they needed, and he moved her to the other room. "Now stay inside, no matter what," he ordered, as he heard a whistle and looked out the window.

"Is somebody here?"

"Yeah, somebody's here all right," he replied, with a smile. "Riff." And, with that, he walked over to her, took her into his arms, and held her close for a moment. "Remember. Positive thinking. I'll be back."

"Positive thinking," she muttered. She smacked him on the back. "Sure."

At that, he grinned, grabbed her chin, and gave her a hard kiss.

"Now for that, I might hold a positive thought for you."

He smirked, then winked. "When we get back, sweetheart."

"*Ha, ha, ha,* maybe not. I could be too pissed at you by then."

"That's all right. I've got your number now." And, with that, he headed out the door. She watched from behind the curtain, as he got into a strange vehicle, and it took off. She wished she had some way of knowing what they were heading into, but what she did know was that it was bound to be bad news all the way. And, with that, she sat down on the bed to wait.

"HOW'D SHE TAKE it?" Riff asked Legend.

"Not easily, but I don't know what she expected."

"Like most women, she probably expected it would go her way," Riff stated, with a laugh.

Legend shook his head. "The last thing I need right now is to worry about her too."

"Do you think she's stashed safely enough here?"

"I hope so," Legend said. "I can't put a cloak or a guard around her and keep my energy steady for what's coming."

Riff considered that and then nodded slowly.

Legend shook his head. "Regardless it's good to know where the lines must be drawn," he noted, feeling unsettled.

Riff nodded. "Hopefully she'll be safe enough there."

"Are you working for Terkel now?" Legend asked Riff.

"I'm still on the fence about it because I'm trying to solve another problem. He's agreed to give me a hand when things ease up, but I just don't know that I have enough to go on to not be wasting their time yet."

Legend stared at him, but Riff just shrugged.

"You could explain a little more," Legend suggested.

"I could," Riff agreed, "and, yeah, it would pass away the drive time, but it won't help us get this asshole. So maybe I'll fill you in later," he muttered. "If you stick around with Terkel anyway."

"They do seem to have their shit together."

"Yeah, I've just never seen anybody have it together quite like they do. Most of the time we're all complete mavericks, but somehow Terk's managed to get this group corralled into some sort of formal organization with a cohesive team. I don't get it."

At that, Legend laughed. "I know, and you're right. We almost never see people like us on teams, but somehow it seems to work with them."

"True. I've never done the whole team thing well, and yet Terk seems to manage it."

"I don't know whether it's a case of good training or the fact that they all came out of government service. I just don't know."

They pondered that as they drove back toward the mansion.

"I took a look at the blueprint," Riff said.

"Okay, good. I suspect all the normal routes will be completely blocked off."

"I would guess that they'll appear to be completely loose and all open, until we get inside. Then they'll be blocked off," he corrected.

"Good point," Legend agreed.

"And you've taken two different routes out of that place, right?" Riff asked.

"Yes, we've gone through the loading zone, and the first time we went down through the basement."

"Right," he muttered. "So next, I would suggest we try to find an entrance or exit to the place that they don't know about."

"Well, if they've spent any amount of time there, they'll know about the obvious ones," Legend noted. "Though there is one that my brother showed me. Down in the basement, there is access to the cold rooms, and the cold rooms have outdoor access, but they're a ways from the house."

"I like it," Riff said, "as long as they haven't got it blocked."

"We'll find that out once we get there." Once again, they parked in the trees, but this time in a completely different location. As they stopped and stared, Legend sent out a query on his senses, but he found nothing and heard nothing. He shrugged. "I'm not getting anything, are you?"

"No, I'm not," Riff replied, "but I suspect it'll be a case of everybody waiting for us to show up, ready to pounce."

"Yep," he muttered. "Let's get this show on the road then."

"Sure, why keep them waiting, right?"

And, with that, they quickly raced through the trees, heading toward the back of the house. When they got within about one hundred yards from the main house, Legend pointed out an old mound off to the side with a plywood door. "That goes into the root cellar and what used to be the old cold vents," he muttered. "From there, it has kind of a tiled accessway into the main part of the house."

They snuck up to it, with no sign of anybody around or even being able to see them. Then they slipped into the old entrance, closing the door behind them. They moved through the tunnel until they reached the house. When they got up to the kitchen, they froze, listening, but there was nothing.

Riff looked over at him with an eyebrow raised, and Legend just shrugged, and they kept on going.

As Legend and Riff headed upstairs, Legend heard voices, probably coming from the office. That only made sense, as that was where Legend had taken everything from. He shouldered the pack that he had, leaving the USBs in the outer pocket, though he'd stripped them clean. He'd removed the bulk of the money but left a little bit, in case they were willing to grab that and run, but he didn't expect that to happen. All the rest of the information had been left at the motel with Blair.

As soon as they hit the main hall, Riff melted into the

shadows, and Legend strolled confidently forward to the office. When he stepped inside, two men looked at him expectantly. He studied them both and nodded. "I guess that's to be expected."

"What's that?" the first one asked, as he pulled the cigar from his mouth. "You didn't really expect your daddy to be here, did you?"

"No, not anymore. At least if the news outlets are worth listening to."

"Well, the news reports are generally wrong, but, in this case, unfortunately, they were correct. Your father was shot, right in the back."

Legend nodded. "Just the way he liked to do it."

"That's what I heard too, but you never know. He could have been faking his death."

"Honestly," the other man added, in a quiet tone, "we waited for the same reason, but I did see him, and he's truly gone."

"It wasn't unexpected," Legend replied, refusing to show any emotion because these guys were looking for that. "Now, what kind of deal are you looking to make? This property belonged to Larry's mother, so it should be his with no question."

"It's also possible the government will seize it."

"That's true, but it's equally possible that won't happen. It'll take a bit of time to sort through this mess."

"Right," said the man with the cigar, "but you know what I want."

"What's that?"

"I want what you took from the safe."

"What would that be?" Legend asked, staring at him. The second man remained silent. Legend had no idea who the second man was, but the first one was the property manager or the business manager who his father had employed for years. "Which one of you is Richard?"

At that, both men laughed.

"It's a name we both use, and it really just means *boss* for us."

"Of course," Legend replied, nodding. "So, what'll it take to have you guys pull the contract on my brother?"

At that, an eyebrow went up on the smoker's face. "You heard about that, did you?"

"Because your guys failed," Legend stated bluntly, "but I'm not interested in keeping Larry safe for the next ten years, while he grows up to be an adult."

"Ten years is a long time. I mean, if he even got a couple more years of life, that would be a huge surprise. He's what, five?"

"No."

"What nine, ten?"

"He's ten," Legend murmured.

"But that could be all for him," the smoker stated, letting Legend just contemplate that for a moment or two. "Well, we told you what we wanted, which is the contents of the safe."

At that, Legend nodded. "So you want the money, not the USB keys?" At that, the men eyed each other and then back at him.

"What keys?"

"You know what keys."

"I'll take the keys," the second man stated. "Make them my payment."

"What? So you can turn around and blackmail the same people?"

He shrugged. "Doesn't matter if I do or not. Those people made the decision when they got themselves into all that trouble in the first place," he stated, with a half laugh.

"What about the contract on my brother?"

"I can pull that," the first man replied, "as long as I get my money."

"What makes you think there was any substantial sum in that safe?"

"Well, there was."

"Sure there *was*, before he put his plans into place."

At that, the smoker frowned.

Somebody stepped up behind Legend, and he stiffened but didn't move. The bag was pulled roughly from his shoulder and tossed toward the two men.

They immediately grabbed it, finding both the cash and the keys. The cash made them frown. "There should have been at least ten times this much."

"There was nothing even close to that." Legend laughed. "You probably know better than I do that my father always traveled with a lot of cash."

"Yeah, he did, didn't he?" He swore as he looked at the money again. "That won't even get us out of the country."

"You don't need his money to get out of the country. Come on. You've been taking good care of yourselves all these years. You're just looking for a final payout."

At that, the other man looked at the smoker and laughed. "Jesus, it's almost like he knows you."

"What do you know?" the smoker asked, his voice turning silky.

"Not much. As you know perfectly well, my father didn't talk to me because he considered me useless to him."

"It's not that you were useless. He just didn't understand

why you were so righteous," he spat, with a disgusted sound. "But when it comes to your brother, you're not quite so righteous, are you? You'll do all kinds of deals to keep him alive. See? That's our best bargaining chip."

"Maybe, and that's *if* you actually have a bargaining chip," he muttered, "which you don't."

"Wow, what makes you think that your brother is safe?"

"I wouldn't be here if he wasn't in a safe place. He is essentially in Fort Knox, and you won't touch him there, but I don't want to sit there and keep him in a place like that until he's an adult. In addition, I'm his guardian, and paperwork has already been taken care of to ensure that, if he dies, it all comes to me, and, if I die, it all goes to charity."

The other guy stared at Legend in shock. "Jesus, he told me that, but I figured you were bluffing,"

"Not bluffing."

"Jesus, why charity?"

"To get you guys off our back," Legend stated, "and any charity is fine by me, which is another aspect of me that my father hated."

The other man nodded. "Yeah, I can see why. Talk about a fucking waste." He glared at him and asked, "So what the hell are you even here for?"

"I want the contract rescinded on my brother," Legend repeated.

"You don't have much in the way of bargaining chips." The smoker pointed at the little bit of stuff on the desk.

"That's not true. You've got the bargaining chips right there."

"But *we* have them. Remember that part. We actually have them here in our hands, so you don't. Therefore, if you don't have anything else to offer, I really don't give a shit. So

I can pop you right now, and your little brother will have nobody."

"He's got a team of people who will look after him," Legend corrected. "His life is fine, but we don't want to sit here and deal with you guys constantly."

"You've already taken out several of my men."

"No, not your men, my father's men. Men willing to turn for a few bucks."

"They didn't turn at all," the one man stated angrily. "However, they were looking for something to call their own, when their wages were no longer getting paid."

"They've been well paid for a long time, just as you guys have," Legend declared. "I know my father would have taken you out if he thought you'd been stealing from him, but I'm pretty sure guys like you steal anyway."

The one guy laughed. "No, that's true, and we got a lot of what we needed over the years. I could probably live just fine, but you know? … You see all this sitting around here, and it's such a big parcel of money that you can't help but want to get your hands on it."

"But you can't now." Legend smiled. "As I said, unless the government decides to seize it, even this house has been signed and sealed. So what becomes of it will all be up to Larry and what he wants to do with it."

"Larry?" he repeated. "God, that kid is even worse than you are. Do you have any idea how much your father hated the fact that his kids were the squeaky-clean type? He hated the fact that you were *special*, as he called it. I have no idea what the fuck that specialty is. You look pretty ordinary to me. As far as he was concerned, power was something that needed to be used."

"And that's what got him shot in the back," Legend noted, with a shrug. "So, it's not as if it did him any good to have that attitude either. Look. I understood my father just fine, but that didn't mean I liked his politics. All I'm here for is to discuss the contract you put out on a little kid."

"You can buy it out," the smoker offered, "just one-quarter of a million dollars for Larry."

"That's nice," Legend replied. "Do you think I have that kind of money?"

"You do because you look after the kid now," he stated, with a flat smile. "So, the answer to that question is obviously yes. You pay that, and we cancel the hit."

Legend eyed him for a long moment, knowing that, even if he did pay, there would never be an end to this. He rubbed the back of his neck, and immediately guns appeared in both men's hands. "Wow, look at that, so much trust."

"No honor among thieves," the two men said at once.

"We've been working with your father for decades to overthrow the government and to take care of business," the smoker began. "Absolutely nothing you can say or do will change how we feel about this. You will now control a ton of money, and we need a ton of money to reestablish ourselves again." They looked at each other, smirks on their faces.

"Is that what you'll do, just set up a whole new war? Another camp of soldiers to come back after the same government?"

"Well, if not this one, another one. It's amazing how many people will pay to have you kick down their government and to put a better one in its place." He shrugged. "It's just what we do."

"Just not well. I mean, you lost this one, so what makes you think anybody'll pay you to win the next one?"

"Because they won't know the difference, because, just

like your father, we can feed them lies."

"So did he actually do this out of political beliefs or because he was being paid?"

"He did it because he believed in it. As for me, I did it because I was being paid." The smoker gave Legend another half smile. "So you see? We don't have the political aspirations that your father did. We were just along for the ride because it's fun."

And that, of course, made them the worst kind of mercenaries because the only language they actually understood was money. "So, power and money, that's it, *huh*? And the ability to kill is what? A nice added bonus?"

"It took a while to get to that point, but you're right. It is kind of a nice bonus when you can take out your opponents without any qualms," the smoker acknowledged. "I mean, the world would be a lot easier to live with, if people were honest about the shit they did and if they knew they would get shot for lying, cheating, and stealing. So what the hell? You wouldn't do it, but the fact of the matter is, everybody does it, yet nobody has to pay for it."

"Including you guys?"

He shrugged. "Yeah, including us, but we don't count because we're the power behind these wars."

"Interesting," Legend muttered. "So, what do you want to do in this situation?"

"Well, you'll arrange … our money. We'll give you a couple days to pull in a nice influx of cash. I think one-quarter of a million should do for us to pull back the contract, and then we'll talk about what else we might need," he noted, with a flat smile.

"Meaning that you have no intention of ever stopping to extort money from me."

"Why would we? You have a massive fortune at your fingertips, and it's a fortune that we feel fully justified in having a part of because we helped in getting it."

"So you say, but this house in particular belonged to Larry's mother. It's the family's ancestral home."

"Yeah, and Larry might very well want it, considering that we killed Larry's mother because your dad was getting a little too fed up with her. She became a problem, so to speak, so we had to take her out. We cleaned up his messes for him." The smoker shrugged. "As I mentioned before, killing just becomes easier and easier all the time."

Legend stiffened at that. "I'll be sure to tell him," he replied, almost with a murderous tone. "At some point in time, he'll need to know the reality of his father's actions in that regard."

"Of course," the smoker agreed, "and then there's you. If you don't think we have leverage to make sure you behave too, you've got a rude awakening in store."

At that, he asked, "What kind of leverage would that be?"

"Well, we have a team already at the motel, picking up your girlfriend," he shared, with a laugh. "So, don't think that you'll be getting off scot-free either. We'll hang on to her, until we get that first one-quarter million, and we'll talk after that."

Such a slimy smile had been added to his tone that Legend knew this would have to end tonight, one way or another, and he knew exactly which way he would vote. It may not make him any better than his father, but, at least, Legend was doing it to save a life.

At the look on Legend's face, the others laughed. "We thought you would feel that way," the smoker stated. "But you know? You just won't have any hope of getting to her in time," he added, with the most sinister smile Legend had ever seen. "Even if you manage to find a way to kill us, saving her still won't happen because, … well, the team was already dispatched with a phone call earlier. I'm just waiting for them to call and to tell me that it's all taken care of." He looked down at the phone, then back at Legend and smiled. "So, what'll it be?" he asked. "Keep her alive or not? Because, you know, I'll give them one order when they phone me, and it'll be on your head either way."

CHAPTER 14

BLAIR PACED THE motel room, not even sure what she was supposed to do, but the longer Legend and Riff were gone, the more agitated she got. Almost immediately, when the guys had pulled out of the motel's parking lot, a sense of wrongness filled her, the sense of something going horribly wrong. The beat-up getaway vehicle Legend and she had arrived here in was still outside, the keys in her pocket.

A part of her yelled that she needed to jump into that sucker and go.

Finally, with her instincts still screaming at her, she grabbed all the bags that she could, and it took her two trips to load the vehicle. By the time she came back for one last look around the motel room, she heard voices coming from outside, and she heard the phrase *catch that bitch*. Immediately she slipped out the window on the far side and went down the fire escape, then raced around to the front and drove off, careful to drive at a slow and steady pace, not wanting anybody to take an interest in her.

As soon as she was out of the parking lot, she gunned it—as much as she could in this old heap—heading back toward the ancestral home. Yet there was absolutely no reason for her to go there, except for the fact that Legend was there. But that also meant that trouble was there as well. Suddenly she wondered what she was doing. What the hell was she doing driving toward trouble, when she should be driving away from it?

At that thought, Terkel's voice slammed into her head. *Exactly, you need to come here.*

"I can't. They're in trouble." When Terk hesitated, she glommed on to that. "You know it. You *know* they're in trouble."

I do know they're in trouble, but having you there won't make it any easier for them.

"Maybe not easier but surely I can do something."

I've got a large team of militia on the way but not for a little bit of time yet.

"So then what? We need somebody to create a distraction?" she asked curiously.

Something like that, but I've already got Riff on it. If you get into the mix, chances are you'll just get hurt.

"Says you," she muttered.

He laughed. *Says me, and, honest to God, why is it that, ever since I've gone private, I have more people wanting to argue with me instead of just doing what I ask?*

"Because we're not used to being part of a team like this, where we're supposed to follow orders when they're wrong."

Are my orders wrong? he asked.

"Yes, at this point in time they are." She didn't know how she knew, but she knew. "Get that team there as fast as you can." And, with that, she pushed him out of her head.

It didn't take anywhere near as long as she thought it would to get close to the mansion, and, knowing that boldness was about the only option she had, she pulled right up to the front door, got out, and slammed the car door hard, yet hid the bags underneath one of the other vehicles, then strode up to the front door. She opened the door and called out, "Well, I'm here."

First came silence and then a scurry of activity, as everybody raced to the front hallway.

She walked inside, took one look at Legend, then smiled. "There you are," she said, and, walking over, she reached up and kissed him hard, but he was stiff, and anger radiated from him. She patted him gently.

Then she turned, faced the other two men, and greeted them. "Ah, and here we go, Richard and Garry," she noted, with a nod. "The two men your father trusted the most."

At that, the pair looked at her, not at all sure just what the heck was going on.

She nodded. "Yeah, you sent some of your friends to the motel room," she began. "I decided I didn't want to talk with them. If you want to talk to me, then you talk to me personally," she declared, glaring at the men. "The only thing you guys understand is power and money."

Legend jerked at that, almost as if it were a phrase he knew well. She turned, looked up at him, then smiled and asked, "Hey, are you okay?"

"I'm fine. You sure don't follow orders, do you?"

She shrugged. "No, not really, not when everything is screaming at me to get the hell out." He nodded at that, then turned and looked at the other men.

"So, now that you don't have her as a hostage, new deal," Legend stated. "You guys rescind the order on Larry's life, and I won't kill you where you stand." At that, they looked at the guns in their hands and then at him without any weapons. He stood there, his hands on his hips, completely nonchalant, as if he didn't care.

"You don't even have a weapon," Richard, the cigar smoker, pointed out.

She frowned at that because he did have two weapons; they'd taken two out of the safe, but she didn't mention that. "He doesn't need a weapon," she stated. "He was just worried earlier about whether I'd been taken or not."

The guys looked at each other, then back at her. "You guys don't even act normal."

"No, we sure don't," she agreed cheerfully. "Now, the question is, will you do your thirty-five years in prison cheerfully, or would you rather take a bullet?" She had said it so abruptly that they looked at her and blinked.

"What are you talking about?" Richard cried out.

"It's like this. We won't tolerate that contract on Larry," she stated. "So, if you don't pull it, we'll just take you down. Afterward we'll put out a news bulletin, saying that you've been captured by the military and that you're talking, revealing your known associates in exchange for a lighter sentence."

At that, Garry blew up furiously. "You know what would happen to us then, don't you?"

"Yep, I sure do," Blair confirmed. "Do you think I give a shit?"

Silence settled over the room. At that, Richard pointed the gun at her. "We were doing just fine before you came along."

"That's why you killed Larry's mother too, wasn't it? It's not that Mr. Kartal wanted her dead, but *you* wanted her dead because she was working at trying to get him to be a better person and to let go of all this. You didn't like her interference, so you're the one who shot her. You probably made Mr. Kartal think that it was his idea, but it was you all along."

Richard stared at her, ... fury making his face work.

"How the hell do you know that?" he roared.

"It's easy," she declared, "and I know all kinds of other shit too. I also know that you have no plans of sharing your largesse with your partner here. You're planning on knocking off Garry before this day is done."

Richard stared at her in shock, while Garry glared at Richard. "What?" Garry asked his partner.

Knowing she had them on their heels, distracted, even divided, she continued. "After all, your men are being hunted now. It was only a matter of time before you would have to whittle down the numbers, and this was a good way to do it. Plus you don't even need the money from Larry because you've been ripping off his father for decades. All a part of the game, and he was okay with it to a degree, as long as you kept it to a reasonable amount. But, after you killed Larry's mother, things didn't go quite so easily between you, and Mr. Kartal was getting a little more worried. He even set up his own private little revenge, just in case."

"What's that?" Richard asked nervously.

She smiled. "I guess you'll have to wait and see."

He stared at her uneasily and then looked at the exit.

"Yeah," Blair taunted, "you should be looking for the damn exit."

Without warning, he raised his gun and fired a bullet at her.

Only she was no longer there; she stood in front of Legend, just slightly off to the side. "Yeah, that worked out well, didn't it?" she asked in a mocking tone.

He glared at her. "What the hell," he cried out. He fired again and again and again, but, each time, he missed. He stared down at the gun, then over at Legend, who just stood there, his hands on his hips. His voice a whisper, clearly in shock, Richard asked, "What are you people?"

She smiled. "We're *special*," she replied in a mocking tone, a word that he had used to describe Larry. "You just have no idea how *very special* we are." She walked up to Richard but looked over at his partner. "Were you ready to die tonight?" she asked in a conversational voice. "Honestly, that was the plan."

Garry shook his head. "No, hell no, I want out of here. In fact, I'm prepared to leave right now and never come back."

"Good choice," she confirmed. "Go out the front door, don't stop, head straight down the driveway, and don't take a vehicle with you."

With that, he booked it for the front door and never slowed down.

She sent Terkel a message about his flight path. Then she turned to Richard. "Put out the call to rescind the order," she ordered.

He shook his head. "You can't make me, even if I don't know what the hell you did to his gun."

"Well, if it's the one left in the safe, that's easy. We fixed it before we left here earlier." She looked over at Legend and smiled. "You think I didn't see you do that, *huh?*"

Legend sighed. "You could let a man have his moment, you know?"

She laughed. "Not Richard, he doesn't get any more moments. If nothing else he should go down for the murder of Larry's mother. However, the fact of the matter is, nobody will even want a trial. They would rather put a bullet in his head and help him disappear, along with the rest of this insurrection nightmare," she shared, with great delight.

"Well, you won't be the one to do it," Richard stated,

his face twisting. "I don't even need a gun to take you guys down." As he spoke, he pulled a knife from a sheath in his boot.

She looked at him and shrugged. "That might cause some damage, but, between the two of us, I think we can do a whole lot more."

All of a sudden came sounds of vehicles coming up the driveway. When Richard twisted suddenly, she nodded. "Yep, that is the sound of your window of opportunity … closing."

He turned to look at her, scowling.

"That's the military here to pick you up," she stated, with a smile. "Now, a wire is about to go out, letting everybody know that you're talking nicely to the military and helping them out for a lighter sentence. You won't get one, and we'll be certain to help out all we can to ensure you go away for a long time. That's under the unlikely scenario that you live to go to prison at all because somebody will cheerfully put a knife in your back between now and what, Sunday, you think?" She faced Legend for a moment, then looked back at Richard. "Do you think you'll live that long?"

Since Sunday was a couple days away, she didn't think Richard would even make it that far.

"No, I don't think he's got a snowball's chance of making it to Saturday, let alone Sunday," Legend shared, his arms coming around her shoulders, pulling her back against him, his fingers squeezing her gently.

"No, I don't think so either," she agreed.

Just then the doors opened, and teams of military raced in. She pointed out Richard. "He's the one you want, gentlemen. He's the one behind the insurrection, the coup, and he has murdered various people all along the line. We can hand over plenty of very interesting paperwork and USBs to help you nail him for it."

"What paperwork?" Richard asked, turning to look at her.

"Well, one of the things we found in the safe was an insurance policy Larry's father had written against you. It's a list of all the people that you took out, some of it for him, but it doesn't really matter who it was for, since it was you who pulled the trigger," she explained. Then she pulled out the one USB key that hadn't gone into the bag and handed it to the military commander, who was staring at her. "You'll find the names and dates are all here," she said.

He took it and smiled, then turned and looked at Richard. "Sounds like you and I need to have a talk."

"If you want to talk to him, you better do it fast, before his cronies find out. Don't forget to make sure everybody knows he's singing like a bird."

"Absolutely, and that should keep as much of this revolution down as we can." Then he ordered Richard to be taken outside.

At that, the commander turned and looked at her. "I have met you somewhere before, haven't I?"

She nodded. "You have, indeed, but it's been a few years."

He pondered that as he headed toward the front door. Then he turned and said, "It was about a little boy who was deathly ill, wasn't it?"

"Yes, it was."

He nodded. "As I recall, you and somebody else did an awful lot to keep him alive."

"Keeping him alive has always been our priority, and that's why we're here today," she explained. "He's just a little boy."

He nodded. "Just make sure he doesn't turn out like his father."

"Not an issue," she declared. "That's the last thing he would ever be."

At that, the commander raised a hand. "Good. Make sure of it." And, with that, he was gone.

Blair turned and there was Riff, standing in the shadows. "You almost look like you're bored," she noted.

He shrugged. "It took a fair bit to actually direct them right here," he replied, "particularly after you sent that idiot outside again. Not to mention the fact that I had to keep your energy up the whole time to avoid those damn bullets."

"Thank you for that," she said, with a big grin. "You really should consider working with Terkel's team full-time."

"Why, so I can deal with more crazies like you?"

"Absolutely," she agreed, with a broad smile. "You do know some female doctor is hassling Terk too, right? About you?"

He stared at her, then groaned. "Of course she is."

"You *will* find the answers regarding your fiancée's murder, but you do need to walk away from it at some point."

"*When* I get answers?" he asked, his gaze flying to her. "What do you even know about it?"

"I don't know a whole lot," she admitted, "but I do know that there is an answer, and it's fairly close, and an awful lot of people want you to find it, so you can get back to the land of the living."

He nodded slowly, his gaze penetrating her. "Anybody in particular?"

"Perhaps," she said, with a smile, as he stared off in the distance. "You know perfectly well that's where you belong, and it's only guilt that's sending you in this other direction." He stiffened, then glared at her. She shrugged. "Yeah, I do know I have a habit of speaking when people don't want me to. Don't worry," she added, with a wave of her hand.

"Will everybody at Terkel's place be like you?"

"I don't know. I haven't been there yet," she said, "but I'm kind of hoping so." There was an almost wistful tone to her voice. "It feels like I've been alone for a very long time."

At that, Legend pulled her back until she leaned against his chest. "Of course this big galoot behind me," she muttered, "is not so different from you. He's had his own demons to deal with, so he's ignored me too."

At that, Riff laughed. "Well, I sure as hell hope you start tormenting him and leave me the hell alone," he noted in disgust.

"I plan to, but you can bet that friend of yours, the doctor, is calling out loud and clear for help," Blair told him, "and when she starts sending signals—"

"She's a megaphone, I know," Riff replied, with a pained expression, "but I can't get her to stop."

"That's because you're not listening. Stopping is one thing. Listening is another."

He snorted. "I'll see you guys back in Cambridge." And, with that, he disappeared into the shadows.

She turned, twisting into Legend's arms.

LEGEND LOOKED DOWN at her and shook his head. "What the hell are you even doing here?"

She laughed. "I fully intended to follow your instructions, honest to God." Then she explained what happened.

He nodded. "Well, I can't really fault that because, when your instincts say you need to make a move, you need to make a move." He pulled her into his arms and just held her close. "Now what?"

"Now, I suggest we grab some real food, some shut-eye, and head to Cambridge. I'm looking forward to seeing Larry again."

Legend chuckled. "Yeah, that's a good point, and we at least need to let them know we're okay."

"No, we don't," she said. "Terkel knows, and he'll pass on the message."

Legend sighed. "It'll be very strange to get used to this many people knowing about everything we do."

"It will. But it'll also be strange to know that you actually have somebody who cares whether you come home or not. But you can handle it. I have faith."

He looked down at her, his grin wry as he asked, "There's really no hope for me, is there?"

"Not one hope in hell," she said, smiling sweetly.

He sighed. "What if I don't want it?"

She stopped, looked up at him. "Do you *not* want it?"

Just enough challenge filled her tone that he tapped her nose. "Of course I want it. I just never believed I could have it."

"But that's the thing," she murmured, "because you can. You really can."

"Promise?"

"Absolutely, and, if we weren't here, I would prove it to you."

"Oh, so you'll prove it to me, will you?" he challenged her, his gaze sparking with interest.

"We could go to my old bedroom here and make a moment of it now."

"God no, anyplace but here."

"Good point," she agreed, "so back to the motel it is, but this time we're picking up food on the way."

"I presume you're hungry," he said, with a sigh.

"I think I'm always hungry, but particularly when I'm burning energy."

As they walked back outside, toward the vehicle, he turned to her. "Did you really have something to do with those bullets?"

"Yeah, I sure did," she admitted. "I can shift air. I just can't stop the gun from firing."

"So, you were taking a chance," he noted, stopping and looking at her. "Those bullets still could have hit you."

"Sure, but they could also have hit you, and I wouldn't let that happen."

He gave a shout of laughter, wrapped an arm around her, and added, "I would say, *Let's go home*, but I'm not sure where home is. So, grab the bags, and go back to the motel. Tomorrow is a whole new day."

CHAPTER 15

FOR ALL THE effort of getting into the motel, by the time Blair and Legend tumbled into their motel room, laughing and giggling like kids, with a bag of takeout in their arms, the only thought Blair had in her mind was about Legend.

He wrapped his arms around her and whispered against her ear, "Food first or …?"

She chuckled, already lifting his T-shirt to slide her hands underneath, feeling the smooth expanse of his bare chest. "You can eat," she murmured. "I'll feast on something else."

He burst out laughing and quickly shucked his clothes, only stopping when she placed her hands on his boxers and slowly lowered them herself. He sucked in his breath, as her hands found him. He whispered, "You're wearing way too many clothes."

"Not for long," she replied quietly, as she slowly slipped his boxers all the way down to his ankles, helping him to step out of them, while she feasted on the proud manhood in front of her. She quickly slid her hands up the back of his thighs and around the inside, stroking and soothing the leg muscles, while watching his erection twitch with each inhaled breath as she got closer and closer to the area he really wanted her to touch.

Slowly she slid her hand over the top of his firm erection, grasping it gently in one hand, sliding her hand down and back up, as her other hand kept exploring. He stood, his stance wide apart, breathing heavily.

"Good Christ, at this rate, it'll be over before it's begun."

She gave him a cheeky look. "Then we'll just have to do it again. I am a teacher, you know, and practice is part of an everyday schedule."

His eyes opened wide, and he looked at her for a moment blankly. Then he started to chuckle and, within seconds, had her picked up and flying through the air, where he tossed her onto the bed. "Yeah, I'm all for any lessons you think you want to teach me, and believe me, I'll be a very attentive pupil," he replied, as he came down on top of her.

"In that case, you really need to start with some basics. You have no clothes on, and I've got way too many, so this just won't work." He waggled his eyebrows, and, with an example of his deftness, she was suddenly stripped down to the buff. She shrieked with laughter. "Oh my, apparently no lessons will be required after all."

"Just the ones that are fun," he noted, as he lowered his head and slowly draped his heavily muscled body atop her frame, giving her every chance to pull back, but she wrapped her arms around his neck and pulled him even closer.

"I waited a long time for you to finally make your way back home again," she murmured.

He nuzzled her nose gently and nodded. "I was always home. I just couldn't quite get my mind wrapped around how it was supposed to work."

"That's because you let that magnificent brain of yours interfere, but there are times when you're just supposed to let things happen."

He smiled, gently kissed her once and then twice, before she protested.

"Now let's do it properly," she ordered.

"Yes, ma'am," he said, and, with a twinkle in his eyes, he lowered his head and kissed her deeply, their tongues warring in remembrance of times gone by.

She sighed against his lips and whispered, "Much better." She wrapped her legs around his hips, pulling him even closer. "I didn't think we would ever get here," she whispered.

"Well, we are now, so we can forget about all that time in between."

She nodded and held him tight, then slowly slid her hands down to his buttocks and dug in her nails. He yelped gently, and she laughed. "That's just in case you think you would spend all of our time here socializing," she murmured.

"Never with you," he noted. "As I recall, you are all about getting to the point."

"Oh, I like to take my time too," she added, "but not after it's taken us this long to get back here again."

"Oh, I can agree with that," he replied, his voice thickening with passion. He used his knees to spread her thighs wide and settled between them.

However, instead of entering her, as she thought he would, he slowly dropped his head and took his time, as he made a pathway down to her breasts, first one and then the other, before slowly slipping down farther and farther.

He spent several moments at the smooth muscles along her abdomen and then at her hips, her belly, his fingers going all the way down to her toes and under her feet. She gasped and giggled, as he slid up the inside of her arch. He smiled, but, just as she relaxed, he dropped his mouth against her plump outer lips and gently suckled. She shuddered, coming apart in his arms, the orgasm striking her so fast and hard that she wasn't even ready for it.

When it came again and then again, she was a bundle of jelly, quivering in his arms, before he finally made his way up and positioned himself at the entrance to her. He looked down at her. "Remember."

As he slowly slid deep inside, she still quivered around him, but she managed to lift her thighs, wrapped them tightly around him, hooking her legs behind his hips, and whispered, "Maybe not. I think you'll have to do better than that."

And, with that, he gave a shout of laughter and drove all the way home. After that first plunge, he was a piston, driving out of control, for his own needs had quickly overtaken him.

She seemed just along for the ride, which was totally fine with her because she was still shuddering from the aftermath of everything that had already happened. And just as he deposited his seed deep within her, another orgasm left her quivering and mindless, as he slowly collapsed beside her.

She whispered, when she finally could, "I don't remember any of that."

"I don't either," he said, holding her close. "I suggest we try it again."

"Later," she whispered, "at least two minutes later."

His warm breath stroked along her neck as he held her close, the tilt of his lips making her smile as he whispered, "That's fine. We do have a lifetime, after all."

"I'm glad to hear that," she whispered. "It seems like we waited forever for this."

"Maybe," he muttered. "I was just stubborn, thinking

that I didn't want to interfere in Larry's world. I couldn't do that to him, and, if you and I had a relationship that didn't work out? Well, … it would affect him and not in a good way. So I walked away and ignored you."

"I get that too, although picking a fight whenever you were around was my way of dealing with that stony wall of silence," she noted. "However, Larry will always be there with us, not between us, and that's the important thing to remember."

He smiled and leaned over. "Are you okay to head to Terkel's place? I've got confirmation that they have a set of rooms for us."

She stopped and looked up at him. "For us?"

His lips twitched. "Yeah, apparently for us. They already knew, and that is something we'll have to get used to. They're apparently very powerful energy workers."

"Meaning, they're also psychics too, I presume," she said hesitantly.

He nodded. "Yes, exactly."

She looked up at him and smiled. "I guess we won't hide anything from each other either, will we?"

"Well, we might hide each other from each other," he noted, with a laugh, "but definitely not from them."

"Got it," she said, and then she smiled. "It's all good, and, yes, I do want to go because they have abilities that we can only dream about, and we need to learn."

"Do we?" he asked, as he gazed down at her. "We would have a more private life if we didn't go there."

"I know, but I think both you and I spent a long time on the outside of having our own family life. So maybe it's time for us to try being inside a family, where we aren't always alone."

"It could get crowded," he warned.

"It could, indeed," she agreed, with a smile. "And a part of me is really looking forward to it, not to mention I think, for Larry, it will be awesome."

"No, I totally agree with you there," Legend said. "For the first time, Larry will have a stable family, maybe way more family than he ever really expected." Legend laughed. "It won't be the kind of place where he gets to isolate himself."

"No, sure won't," she agreed, "but I think it will be good for all of us."

"Well, in that case, we'll head over there tomorrow."

She shook her head. "No, how about the day after?" she asked, wrapping her arms around him. "You can tell them that we'll be busy tomorrow."

"Busy doing what?" he asked, waggling his eyebrows.

"Exactly," she murmured. "Anything and everything we want. We'll see them the day after." And, with that, she pulled him down again, and murmured, "I promise to keep you busy, and you definitely won't get bored."

As he lowered his head, he whispered, "Never with you in my arms, sweetheart, never with you." And he sealed his words with a kiss.

EPILOGUE

AS LEGEND AND Blair drove up to Guardian headquarters, she stared and gasped. "Oh my God, it really is a castle, isn't it?"

Legend laughed. "Not only a castle, it's a massive castle." He looked somewhat excited himself. "They're still trying to work their way through all the logistics of updating it."

She frowned at him and asked, "It does have indoor plumbing though, right?"

He grinned. "It does, indeed, have indoor plumbing. In fact, I understand the bathrooms have been massively updated and a few other things as well. ... So, some tolerance and patience will be required, but that will work both ways. We'll need to make a ton of adjustments, and so will they."

She nodded, as she got out. "It's so huge."

"It is, and they own acres and acres here, so lots of ground for you to explore. You can take Larry out for walks and all kinds of adventures." He grabbed his bags, and she grabbed hers, and they started for the front door.

Before they ever had a chance to reach for it, Larry came barreling out with all the exuberance a ten-year-old could manage. He threw himself first into her arms and then into Legend's. "There you are," he screamed.

She laughed, the three of them in a three-way hug, as she

kissed Larry on the cheek. "Sounds like you're having a blast."

"Oh my gosh, it's amazing. Can we stay here? Can we stay?"

"Well, I'm not positive about that, but we'll see."

He looked up at her beseechingly. "Please, there's so much I can learn. You have no idea."

"Yeah, that's just because you know that Clary is here along with Little Calum."

"Well, that too," he agreed, with a big grin. He threw his arms around her neck and hugged her close. "I'm really happy that you guys are together too. It'll be almost like a real family."

"It *is* a real family," she stated. "No matter what it seemed like before, this is the real deal."

He looked from one to the other and got choked up. "You promise?"

"I promise," Legend vowed, wrapping an arm around her shoulders and then around Larry's. "Now, shall we go in and talk to the rest of the team?"

"Yeah, you don't even know who's all here," Larry added, "and you won't believe all the baby bumps." He looked at her and asked, "Have you got a baby in there yet?"

She flushed. "No, I hope not," she replied, embarrassed.

"Well, I wouldn't give it very long," Larry declared, "because you will be if you stay here."

"Why is that?"

As they walked inside behind him, they saw several of the women coming out of the kitchen with plates of food, only to stop and look at the newcomers. Blair saw the baby bumps, then she looked back at Legend. "What the hell?" she whispered.

"I have no idea," he muttered. He turned to Terkel, and there stood Brody. "Funny how nobody mentioned that aspect," he said to Brody.

Brody laughed. "Well, we're trying to work on that aspect," he replied, "so we'll give you some pointers now that you're here. However, at the moment, you're the only couple who isn't in the family way." Then he stopped, chuckled, and asked, "Or are you?"

She glared at him. "I better not be."

He shrugged. "We all thought we weren't either, but it's apparently a hazard of this kind of energy."

"Okay, that's definitely a little disconcerting." Blair walked further inside and was introduced to the group of people here. Some she knew of and some she didn't, but the first one to greet her was Clary.

Clary walked over, gave her a gentle hug, and said, "So glad to have you here. Larry has been an absolute treat to have around."

At that, Blair laughed. "And he tells me there's so much he can still learn that he definitely needs to stay."

"Well, it's a good thing you're staying then, isn't it?" Clary teased.

Blair smiled. "Well, at least for a while."

"Nope, no *at least for a while* nonsense," Terkel replied, as he assessed her with one quick clean look and nodded. "You'll do just fine."

She stared at him. "And you are?"

He grinned. "Terkel, grand master of this insane household."

She nodded. "Nice to meet you. I'm glad to know that you're an actual person and not just a voice in my head."

At that, everybody burst out laughing.

"Yeah," Terk confirmed. "I'm definitely a voice in your head. I am also a real person, and we will all, at one time or another, be voices in your head."

Another woman walked up and added, "One of the first things we'll show you is how to get some privacy and peace and quiet around this place. In the meantime, we have an apartment for you."

Terkel, getting to business right away, stated, "We also have another job, although this one is a little different."

"Aren't they all?" somebody quipped. "I'm Gage, by the way," he told Legend and Blair. Gage sat down with a cup of coffee and asked Terk, "What's going on?"

"Bullard called. He has a woman who's apparently got some psychic ability, and, at the same time, he says that his wife is in trouble."

At that, another woman came up to Terk and wrapped her arms around him, saying, "In that case, you know what to do. We owe him ..."

Terkel nodded. "Yeah, I just have to come up with somebody to go help Bullard." Terk looked around at all the people gathered in the room.

"I'm not doing anything at the moment," said one man, leaning against the wall.

At that, Blair turned and recognized Riff. "You seem to be nowhere and everywhere," she said.

He nodded, giving her a lazy smile. "Yeah, that's me." Riff looked over at Terkel. "Bojan is already in Africa."

Terkel's gaze sharpened, and then he almost zoned out, right in front of them. Soon he nodded. "That would work perfectly," he said in a very soft whisper.

"You want to contact Bojan, or will I?" Riff asked.

"It'll have to be me," Terkel said, "but you might want

to contact Bojan and tell him that I'll be calling."

"You think that'll make a bit of difference? He already knows."

"Yeah, he knows, but it might be easier if he knows that it's coming from you first."

At that, Riff laughed. "Okay, and what's the time frame on this deal for Bullard?"

"Well, how quickly can you get over there?"

"I can be there early in the morning, probably," Riff estimated. He glanced at Terkel and all the others. "Unless somebody else wants to go."

"No, this one's all about you," Terk noted.

"It won't be all about me. It'll be about Bojan," Riff stated.

"And Lacy," Terkel added.

At that, Riff's gaze narrowed. "Lacy?"

"Yeah, the psychic who's been warning Terkel," Gage confirmed.

"The university student in med school in Africa who has been working with Leia," Terk added.

Riff nodded. *"Lacy and Bojan."*

"Perfect," Terkel said. "Tell Bojan I want to talk with him and soon."

And, with that, Riff nodded. "I'll go grab my bag."

This concludes Book 2 of Terk's Guardians: Legend.

Read about Bojan: Terk's Guardians, Book 3

Terk's Guardians: Bojan (Book #3)

Haunted by a painful and unimaginable past, Bojan sought refuge in his work to keep the memories—and Lacy—at bay. But, when she raises the alarm over Bullard's family, Bojan is forced to step into fray. Bullard is particularly wary of these "special" skills, except for those of Terk's team. Plus ignoring the offer of these skills can be dangerous—especially when a threat involves his family.

Lacy is helping the heavily pregnant Leia in the medical clinic, yet can't ignore the danger she sees. But triggering an alarm requires Terk's special brand of help, who then tags Bojan to step up and to handle it. Lacy had no idea Bojan would return to her in the near future. Maybe in some distant future? So finding him in the kitchen one morning is unexpected. Still, now is the time for assistance. She just doesn't know what help Bojan can offer. Or is *prepared* to offer …

Particularly as things go from bad to worse.

Find Book 3 here!

To find out more visit Dale Mayer's website.

https://geni.us/DMSBojan

Author's Note

Thank you for reading Legend: Terk's Guardians, Book 2! If you enjoyed the book, please take a moment and leave a short review.

Dear reader,

I love to hear from readers, and you can contact me at my website: www.dalemayer.com or at my Facebook author page. To be informed of new releases and special offers, sign up for my newsletter or follow me on BookBub. And if you are interested in joining Dale Mayer's Reader Group, here is the Facebook sign up page. http://geni.us/DaleMayerFBGroup

Cheers,
Dale Mayer

About the Author

Dale Mayer is a *USA Today* best-selling author, best known for her SEALs military romances, her Psychic Visions series, and her Lovely Lethal Garden cozy series. Her contemporary romances are raw and full of passion and emotion (Broken But … Mending, Hathaway House series). Her thrillers will keep you guessing (Kate Morgan, By Death series), and her romantic comedies will keep you giggling (*It's a Dog's Life*, a stand-alone novella; and the Broken Protocols series, starring Charming Marvin, the cat).

Dale honors the stories that come to her—and some of them are crazy, break all the rules and cross multiple genres!

To go with her fiction, she also writes nonfiction in many different fields, with books available on résumé writing, companion gardening, and the US mortgage system. All her books are available in print and ebook format.

Connect with Dale Mayer Online

Dale's Website – www.dalemayer.com
Twitter – @DaleMayer
Facebook Page – geni.us/DaleMayerFBFanPage
Facebook Group – geni.us/DaleMayerFBGroup
BookBub – geni.us/DaleMayerBookbub
Instagram – geni.us/DaleMayerInstagram
Goodreads – geni.us/DaleMayerGoodreads
Newsletter – geni.us/DaleNews

Also by Dale Mayer

Published Adult Books:

Shadow Recon
Magnus, Book 1
Rogan, Book 2
Egan, Book 3
Barret, Book 4
Whalen, Book 5
Nikolai, Book 6

Bullard's Battle
Ryland's Reach, Book 1
Cain's Cross, Book 2
Eton's Escape, Book 3
Garret's Gambit, Book 4
Kano's Keep, Book 5
Fallon's Flaw, Book 6
Quinn's Quest, Book 7
Bullard's Beauty, Book 8
Bullard's Best, Book 9
Bullard's Battle, Books 1–2
Bullard's Battle, Books 3–4
Bullard's Battle, Books 5–6
Bullard's Battle, Books 7–8

Terkel's Team

Damon's Deal, Book 1
Wade's War, Book 2
Gage's Goal, Book 3
Calum's Contact, Book 4
Rick's Road, Book 5
Scott's Summit, Book 6
Brody's Beast, Book 7
Terkel's Twist, Book 8
Terkel's Triumph, Book 9

Terk's Guardians

Radar, Book 1
Legend, Book 2
Bojan, Book 3

Kate Morgan

Simon Says… Hide, Book 1
Simon Says… Jump, Book 2
Simon Says… Ride, Book 3
Simon Says… Scream, Book 4
Simon Says… Run, Book 5
Simon Says… Walk, Book 6
Simon Says… Forgive, Book 7

Hathaway House

Aaron, Book 1
Brock, Book 2
Cole, Book 3
Denton, Book 4
Elliot, Book 5
Finn, Book 6

Gregory, Book 7
Heath, Book 8
Iain, Book 9
Jaden, Book 10
Keith, Book 11
Lance, Book 12
Melissa, Book 13
Nash, Book 14
Owen, Book 15
Percy, Book 16
Quinton, Book 17
Ryatt, Book 18
Spencer, Book 19
Timothy, Book 20
Urban, Book 21
Hathaway House, Books 1–3
Hathaway House, Books 4–6
Hathaway House, Books 7–9

The K9 Files
Ethan, Book 1
Pierce, Book 2
Zane, Book 3
Blaze, Book 4
Lucas, Book 5
Parker, Book 6
Carter, Book 7
Weston, Book 8
Greyson, Book 9
Rowan, Book 10
Caleb, Book 11
Kurt, Book 12

Tucker, Book 13
Harley, Book 14
Kyron, Book 15
Jenner, Book 16
Rhys, Book 17
Landon, Book 18
Harper, Book 19
Kascius, Book 20
Declan, Book 21
Bauer, Book 22
The K9 Files, Books 1–2
The K9 Files, Books 3–4
The K9 Files, Books 5–6
The K9 Files, Books 7–8
The K9 Files, Books 9–10
The K9 Files, Books 11–12

Lovely Lethal Gardens

Arsenic in the Azaleas, Book 1
Bones in the Begonias, Book 2
Corpse in the Carnations, Book 3
Daggers in the Dahlias, Book 4
Evidence in the Echinacea, Book 5
Footprints in the Ferns, Book 6
Gun in the Gardenias, Book 7
Handcuffs in the Heather, Book 8
Ice Pick in the Ivy, Book 9
Jewels in the Juniper, Book 10
Killer in the Kiwis, Book 11
Lifeless in the Lilies, Book 12
Murder in the Marigolds, Book 13
Nabbed in the Nasturtiums, Book 14

Offed in the Orchids, Book 15
Poison in the Pansies, Book 16
Quarry in the Quince, Book 17
Revenge in the Roses, Book 18
Silenced in the Sunflowers, Book 19
Toes up in the Tulips, Book 20
Uzi in the Urn, Book 21
Victim in the Violets, Book 22
Whispers in the Wisteria, Book 23
Lovely Lethal Gardens, Books 1–2
Lovely Lethal Gardens, Books 3–4
Lovely Lethal Gardens, Books 5–6
Lovely Lethal Gardens, Books 7–8
Lovely Lethal Gardens, Books 9–10

Psychic Visions Series

Tuesday's Child
Hide 'n Go Seek
Maddy's Floor
Garden of Sorrow
Knock Knock…
Rare Find
Eyes to the Soul
Now You See Her
Shattered
Into the Abyss
Seeds of Malice
Eye of the Falcon
Itsy-Bitsy Spider
Unmasked
Deep Beneath
From the Ashes

Stroke of Death
Ice Maiden
Snap, Crackle…
What If…
Talking Bones
String of Tears
Inked Forever
Insanity
Psychic Visions Books 1–3
Psychic Visions Books 4–6
Psychic Visions Books 7–9

By Death Series
Touched by Death
Haunted by Death
Chilled by Death
By Death Books 1–3

Broken Protocols – Romantic Comedy Series
Cat's Meow
Cat's Pajamas
Cat's Cradle
Cat's Claus
Broken Protocols 1-4

Broken and… Mending
Skin
Scars
Scales (of Justice)
Broken but… Mending 1-3

Glory
Genesis

Tori

Celeste

Glory Trilogy

Biker Blues

Morgan: Biker Blues, Volume 1

Cash: Biker Blues, Volume 2

SEALs of Honor

Mason: SEALs of Honor, Book 1

Hawk: SEALs of Honor, Book 2

Dane: SEALs of Honor, Book 3

Swede: SEALs of Honor, Book 4

Shadow: SEALs of Honor, Book 5

Cooper: SEALs of Honor, Book 6

Markus: SEALs of Honor, Book 7

Evan: SEALs of Honor, Book 8

Mason's Wish: SEALs of Honor, Book 9

Chase: SEALs of Honor, Book 10

Brett: SEALs of Honor, Book 11

Devlin: SEALs of Honor, Book 12

Easton: SEALs of Honor, Book 13

Ryder: SEALs of Honor, Book 14

Macklin: SEALs of Honor, Book 15

Corey: SEALs of Honor, Book 16

Warrick: SEALs of Honor, Book 17

Tanner: SEALs of Honor, Book 18

Jackson: SEALs of Honor, Book 19

Kanen: SEALs of Honor, Book 20

Nelson: SEALs of Honor, Book 21

Taylor: SEALs of Honor, Book 22

Colton: SEALs of Honor, Book 23

Troy: SEALs of Honor, Book 24
Axel: SEALs of Honor, Book 25
Baylor: SEALs of Honor, Book 26
Hudson: SEALs of Honor, Book 27
Lachlan: SEALs of Honor, Book 28
Paxton: SEALs of Honor, Book 29
Bronson: SEALs of Honor, Book 30
Hale: SEALs of Honor, Book 31
SEALs of Honor, Books 1–3
SEALs of Honor, Books 4–6
SEALs of Honor, Books 7–10
SEALs of Honor, Books 11–13
SEALs of Honor, Books 14–16
SEALs of Honor, Books 17–19
SEALs of Honor, Books 20–22
SEALs of Honor, Books 23–25

Heroes for Hire

Levi's Legend: Heroes for Hire, Book 1
Stone's Surrender: Heroes for Hire, Book 2
Merk's Mistake: Heroes for Hire, Book 3
Rhodes's Reward: Heroes for Hire, Book 4
Flynn's Firecracker: Heroes for Hire, Book 5
Logan's Light: Heroes for Hire, Book 6
Harrison's Heart: Heroes for Hire, Book 7
Saul's Sweetheart: Heroes for Hire, Book 8
Dakota's Delight: Heroes for Hire, Book 9
Tyson's Treasure: Heroes for Hire, Book 10
Jace's Jewel: Heroes for Hire, Book 11
Rory's Rose: Heroes for Hire, Book 12
Brandon's Bliss: Heroes for Hire, Book 13
Liam's Lily: Heroes for Hire, Book 14

SEALs of Steel

The Final Reveal: SEALs of Steel, Book 8
SEALs of Steel, Books 1–4
SEALs of Steel, Books 5–8
SEALs of Steel, Books 1–8

The Mavericks

Kerrick, Book 1
Griffin, Book 2
Jax, Book 3
Beau, Book 4
Asher, Book 5
Ryker, Book 6
Miles, Book 7
Nico, Book 8
Keane, Book 9
Lennox, Book 10
Gavin, Book 11
Shane, Book 12
Diesel, Book 13
Jerricho, Book 14
Killian, Book 15
Hatch, Book 16
Corbin, Book 17
Aiden, Book 18
The Mavericks, Books 1–2
The Mavericks, Books 3–4
The Mavericks, Books 5–6
The Mavericks, Books 7–8
The Mavericks, Books 9–10
The Mavericks, Books 11–12

Standalone Novellas

It's a Dog's Life
Riana's Revenge
Second Chances

Published Young Adult Books:

Family Blood Ties Series

Vampire in Denial
Vampire in Distress
Vampire in Design
Vampire in Deceit
Vampire in Defiance
Vampire in Conflict
Vampire in Chaos
Vampire in Crisis
Vampire in Control
Vampire in Charge
Family Blood Ties Set 1–3
Family Blood Ties Set 1–5
Family Blood Ties Set 4–6
Family Blood Ties Set 7–9
Sian's Solution, A Family Blood Ties Series Prequel
    Novelette

Design series

Dangerous Designs
Deadly Designs
Darkest Designs
Design Series Trilogy

Standalone

In Cassie's Corner
Gem Stone (a Gemma Stone Mystery)
Time Thieves

Published Non-Fiction Books:

Career Essentials

Career Essentials: The Résumé
Career Essentials: The Cover Letter
Career Essentials: The Interview
Career Essentials: 3 in 1